MW00424333

# OPERATION GET HER BACK

---

## THE JETTY BEACH SERIES BOOK 4

## CLAIRE KINGSLEY

Always Have LLC

Edited by Larks and Katydids

Cover by Kari March Designs

Published by Always Have, LLC

ISBN: 9781797052311

Previously published as Must Be Home: A Jetty Beach Romance

www.clairekingsleybooks.com

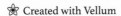 Created with Vellum

## ABOUT THIS BOOK

*Operation Get Her Back was originally published as Must Be Home: A Jetty Beach Romance.*

**She's the most important mission of his life**

I know two things with absolute certainty. Second chances don't come easy. And I'm going to marry Emma Parker.

Ten years ago, I was troubled and angry, looking for an outlet for my rage. To protect the people I love, I made the choice to join the Marines—and leave the love of my life behind.

Emma moved on. But now we're both back in our home-town, and I'm determined to earn her forgiveness. To show her we belong together. I've made loving her my mission, and I'm determined not to fail.

# 1

## EMMA

The cork on the champagne bottle comes off with a pop. I don't have any champagne flutes, so I fill a regular wine glass. Full. Why not? I might be celebrating alone, but celebrate I will.

I stopped at a fancy bakery on the way home and bought myself a slice of chocolate cheesecake. It looks positively decadent: rich brown with a shiny drizzle of dark chocolate criss-crossing the top. A single mint leaf holds a fresh raspberry for a little pop of color. So pretty. I felt like treating myself, and this is just the thing. After all, it isn't every day that your divorce is final.

All the paperwork is signed, recorded, and whatever else they had to do to get me my freedom. It's been a long year, from the moment I packed a bag and walked out on my life, to this one. The moment when my life begins again.

We all make mistakes when we're young. Unfortunately, mine included a legally binding contract and a promise to stay with Wyatt for the rest of our lives. I knew, even when I was saying my vows, that it was a mistake. That probably makes me a terrible person. I spent the entire reception wondering how long I could hold out. Could I really make a life with him? Would this last?

Spoiler: it didn't.

I bring my party for one over to the tiny kitchen table and sit. I try not to be disappointed that I'm alone in my crappy apartment while I do this. I've heard of women throwing divorce parties—going out with their girlfriends to male strip shows and getting drunk together. I would love to go out and do something silly or crazy, let loose a little. But that sort of thing would require girlfriends to go out with, and being married to Wyatt wasn't conducive to having friends. He didn't like any of my friends, and in my quest to keep the peace, I let those relationships drift away.

I let a lot of things drift away. Friends. Family. Myself.

I take a sip of champagne. It was cheap, but it's decent. The slice of cheesecake cost almost as much as the bubbly. I take a bite and close my eyes, letting out a soft groan. Worth every penny. It's smooth and creamy, the chocolate flavor so rich. It's the best thing I've eaten in a long time.

I think about what Wyatt would say if he saw me drinking champagne and eating chocolate cheesecake. Probably something shitty about letting myself go. Then he'd laugh and act like it was a joke, and accuse me of being too sensitive when I got mad about it.

Fuck that guy.

I take a gulp of the champagne. Maybe I should have bought something stronger. Of course, I'm fairly broke, so even the champagne and cheesecake were a splurge. Lawyers are not cheap, and Wyatt fought me every step of the way. Because of course he did. I wanted nothing from him—not the car, the housewares, the furniture. He could keep it all, as far as I was concerned. All I wanted was my freedom. I wanted my name back, and a chance to have a life without walking on eggshells, tiptoeing around a moody bastard all the time. In the end, he couldn't stop me from divorcing him. By the look on his face the last time I saw him in court, I think he was pretty shocked by that fact. He really thought he could keep me.

No one can. Not now. Not ever. I am officially done with men.

I take my time with the cheesecake and pour another glass of champagne. It's a Thursday, so technically I have to work tomorrow, but luckily I work from home. I'm a copy editor for a company that builds websites—a job I got and kept for a year before Wyatt knew about it. He didn't want me to work, and in the beginning I thought putting effort into the marriage meant doing what he wanted, so I went along with it. I was such an idiot. Luckily, I was able to leverage my English degree into the job that ultimately made leaving him possible.

The second glass of champagne goes down quicker than the first. I flip through some shows on TV, only half paying attention. I figure champagne doesn't keep very well, so I get up to treat myself to another glass. While I'm out there, I check the bowl I keep underneath the sink cabinet, to make sure it isn't full. Stupid leak. Stupid apartment. This place has been a nightmare since I moved in, and they still haven't fixed half the problems.

My job is going well, and that was the first step in my plan to reclaim my life. Leaving Wyatt and getting a place to live was the second. This apartment isn't much, but it's mine and I don't have to share it with anyone. That's progress. Now that the divorce is official, I need to start thinking about what comes next. Project Get Emma Back should be in full swing, but I'm not sure if I know what that means. I was twenty-one when I got married, and still trying to figure out who I was. I spent the next six years trying to be who I thought Wyatt wanted me to be.

Now I'm honestly not sure who I am.

A sharp knock at the door makes me jump, and champagne sloshes out over my jeans. Shit. I take a deep breath to steady myself. It's seven o'clock on a Thursday. Who would be here?

Oh god. Did Wyatt find out where I live?

I'm not hiding from him, exactly. He was a dick to live with, but he's not the dangerous type. But I like the feeling that he doesn't know where I am. Plus, I have nothing more to say to him. If I never see him again, it'll be too soon.

I could pretend I'm not home and hope whoever it is goes away. But it could also be building maintenance; in addition to the leaky sink, I have a list of other things they've been promising to fix. This place is literally one step removed from a fucking crack house, and the neighbors smoke so much pot I'm pretty sure I've been high at least a dozen times since I moved in. But it's cheap, and not in a completely horrible neighborhood. If it's a maintenance guy, I should probably answer the door.

I take another breath and go to the front door. It's all of four or five steps from the couch. My apartment is beyond tiny. If it's Wyatt, I'll simply tell him to go away, and close the door. He can bang on it all he wants, I don't have to let him in. And if it *is* maintenance, I can give him an earful about the wretched state of this shithole.

I pull the door open—fast, like ripping off a Band-Aid. No one. The doorstep is empty, and there's no sign of anyone on the stairs. I poke my head out and look around, but I don't see anyone.

That's weird.

I'm just about to close the door when I realize there's a folded piece of paper taped to the outside. I let out the breath I didn't realize I was holding. Way to get worked up over nothing, Emma.

It's probably an advertisement. People flood this apartment complex with fliers all the time. After closing the door and making sure it's locked, I grab my champagne and sit down to check this out. I unfold the paper and see the apartment logo at the top. My eyes dart across the page, my stomach clenching with every word.

*Infestation.*

*Insects.*

*Hazardous.*

*Vacate the premises.*

I have to be out of my apartment for at least a week? Starting tomorrow? Son of a bitch, they must be joking. Where am I supposed to go? They can't just kick me out like this. I don't care if they'll prorate my rent; I need a place to sleep.

I slump down on the couch, the letter falling from my listless fingers. Shit. This is not the first time this stupid apartment has had issues. First it was the plumbing. Then the roof leaked. They made me live without power for three days when something happened to the electricity. And now this? I really need to get out of here.

But I'm not sure where to go. I don't exactly have friends I can call up and ask to crash on their couch. I could rent a hotel, but I don't think I can afford it. Not yet. Getting divorced is freaking expensive.

That leaves family. I could stay with my mom. But she moved into a small condo a few years ago, and she doesn't have a lot of room. Plus, being in close quarters with my mother for an extended period of time (as in, more than an hour) is akin to torture. That leaves one person: Gabriel.

I bring up my brother's number and give him a call.

"Hi, Sis," he says. "You caught me with about two minutes before I have to go. What's up?"

Gabriel is the head chef at the Ocean Mark, a beautiful fine dining restaurant out in Jetty Beach, the town where we grew up. He lives and breathes his job.

"Okay, I'll do this quick. I have to be out of my apartment while they spray for bugs or something. I don't have anywhere else to go."

"Say no more, Emma," he says. "You know you can stay here anytime. I'm hardly ever home, anyway."

"Thanks, Gabe," I say.

"When?"

"Tomorrow."

"Okay," he says. "If I'm at work, let yourself in. And come up to the restaurant. I'll feed you."

I smile. Gabe's cooking is amazing. "I'll take you up on that."

"Good," he says. "See you then."

I hang up with a sigh. My brother is a great guy, and staying at his place won't be so bad. It's the town I'm dreading.

I hate Jetty Beach, with a seething passion that is probably not healthy. I lived there most of my life, but I avoid going back as much as possible. It's been years since I spent more than a day there. Even when I first left Wyatt, I didn't go home to my mom's, or to Gabriel's. I paid for a hotel those first few nights, and was happy to do it. It meant I didn't have to go home.

And now I have to go back?

I close my eyes and lean against the couch cushions.

There's nothing actually wrong with the town, it just holds too many memories—both good and bad. The bad ones came last, and things ended so horribly that I associate all that pain with the place. Every time I drive through that stupid little beach town, all I can see is him.

All I can see is Hunter.

## 2

## HUNTER

*I* hit the punching bag, feeling the force reverberate through my arm, across my back. I step to the side and hit again. Sweat drips down my bare chest, runs in rivulets down my back. I may not be able to run anymore, but I'll be damned if I'm going to let myself get out of shape. My breath comes fast, a jolt of adrenaline coursing through me. Slam. My fist hits with a low thud and the chain clinks.

I drop to the ground and knock out twenty push-ups. It's late afternoon, and this is my second workout today, but I felt too restless to sit around.

My phone rings, so I get up to answer it. "Hi, Mom."

"Hi, Hunter," she says. "Can you pick up some bread on your way over tonight?"

Family dinner. "Sure, what kind?"

"French."

"You got it."

"Thanks, honey," she says. "I'll see you in a couple hours."

"Yeah, Mom, see you then."

I hang up and grab a towel to wipe off my face. Technically, Maureen isn't my mom, but in every way that matters, she is. My dad took off when I was a baby, and I was not an easy child. My mother was single, working two jobs, and the Jacobsens became my second family. I spent more time at their house than I did at my own, going there after school and staying until my mom got off work. They bought their younger son Ryan bunk beds so I had a place to sleep when I stayed over—which was about half the time.

Then my mother got sick, and I hardly ever went home.

Maureen and Ed took care of me while my mom went through chemo. And when it didn't work, and cancer took her, I just stayed with them. I was thirteen at the time, and didn't have any other relatives. There was never a formal adoption—and I've always kept my last name, Evans, mostly to honor my mother—but Maureen was mom.

I didn't actually call her Mom when I was a kid. I never felt like I had a right to. Despite the way they took me in without question, and loved me as much as they loved Cody and Ryan, I felt like an outsider. They introduced me as their son, but I called them Maureen and Ed until the day I left home to join the Marines.

The first time I called her Mom, I was an adult. It was the day I called and asked if I could come back. I was in the hospital, recovering from surgery after a car accident when I was serving overseas. I knew a medical discharge was coming. It was my third surgery, and the doctors had told me I wouldn't ever get back to where I was before. I lay there, staring at the harsh fluorescent lights above the bed, and knew it was time I faced my past. I'd left them without a word, sneaking out of the house late at night, leaving nothing but a note.

Nine years later, it was time. I called Maureen.

*Mom, can I please come home?*

She cried. I cried, and I can admit that without the slightest bit of shame. I was battered and broken and heart-sick. It was time to go home.

To my absolute amazement, the Jacobsens welcomed me back. Okay, so Ryan hit me the first time he saw me, but it was no less than I deserved. Once we had a chance to hash things out, both of the Jacobsen brothers were glad I was home. And I've spent the last year or so trying to repay the debt I owe them, knowing I'll never be able to.

I figure a shower is in order, since I'm sweaty as hell. I pull my t-shirt back on and head out to my truck. I live in town, but I have a big piece of property outside Jetty Beach. It's where I work, and I've built a gym out in the shop. I like to come out here, even when I'm not working. It's peaceful. But I shouldn't show up to dinner smelling like a dirty sock, so I head back to my place and clean up.

About an hour later, I drive out to my parents' house, half dreading dinner. I'll never get tired of Mom's cooking, so the weekly family get-togethers have that going for them. But since Ryan got married last month, and Cody got engaged, I feel like the seventh wheel. Ryan and Nicole are still disgusting in their starry-eyed newlywed bliss, and Cody and Clover are embarrassing with how much they touch and kiss each other, even in front of our folks. I always wind up sitting next to Mom, talking with her about her garden, deflecting questions about my love life, while I try to ignore the lovey-dovey brigade at the table.

It's pouring down rain, which isn't that uncommon for Jetty Beach, even in July. I go inside and find everyone in the kitchen. Mom's taking a big batch of lasagna out of the oven, filling the house with the smell of baked cheese. My mouth waters. I think I can handle my brothers' PDA if I get to eat that for dinner tonight.

"Hey, Son," Dad says. My heart still swells a little when he calls me that. He always has, ever since my mother died. Just like Cody and Ryan. When I was younger, I thought he was harder on me than he was on them, but looking back, I needed it. I still feel guilty for how much I resented them in those days.

"Hey, Dad," I say. "Mom, this smells amazing."

"Did you bring the bread?" Mom asks.

I set the bag with four loaves of French bread on the counter. "Of course."

"Good boy," Mom says, and pats my cheek.

The rest of us finish setting the table and bringing the food over while my mom toasts the bread in the oven. When everything is ready, we all sit down. Because of the weather, we're inside at the big dining table next to the kitchen, rather than on the rooftop deck. Rain patters against the tall windows, partially obscuring the view of the beach. Like always, I sit next to Mom, and steel myself to listen to her lament about what the rain is doing to her tomatoes.

We pass the food around, loading up our plates.

"So," Mom says, passing the bread to Nicole, "when can we expect our first grandbaby?"

Nicole's face goes scarlet, and she almost drops the bread basket.

"Mom!" Ryan says. "Really?"

Cody bursts out laughing. I have to hold my hand over my mouth to keep from snickering.

"What?" Mom asks. "You've been married for a month. That's not an unreasonable question."

"Actually," Ryan says, "it's a very unreasonable question."

Nicole looks like she wants to die. I meet her eyes and try to give her a reassuring look.

"I'm not putting any pressure on you, honey," Mom says. "I'm only curious."

"Okay, well, maybe you can be curious about something else," Ryan says. "So, Cody—I hear you and Clover are thinking about eloping and not having a wedding at all."

I pretend to cough to cover my laughter. We are in rare form tonight.

"What?" Mom turns to Cody, and gives him her interrogation face. "You don't want a wedding?"

Cody glares at Ryan. "We haven't decided anything yet. We're just talking about our options."

It wouldn't surprise me in the least if Cody and Clover run off to Vegas, although that's almost too normal. Clover is sweet, but she's kind of nuts. I'm half-expecting her to announce they'll be getting married in the center of a stone circle in Europe or something.

"Well, for heaven's sake," Mom says. "No wedding? It doesn't have to be big. But you have to have a wedding. Don't you want to celebrate with your family?"

"Let's just not worry about it right now. We haven't even set a date." Cody's eyes shift to me. "Speaking of dates, Hunter, are you still seeing that girl you were talking about?"

Of course he went there.

Mom turns her bright-eyed gaze on me. "Hunter, you're seeing someone?"

Ryan is stifling laughter now.

"No, I'm not seeing anyone," I say. "I went out with someone a couple of times, but we didn't really hit it off."

"Oh, well that's good," Mom says.

Everyone turns toward her.

"What?" I ask. "Why is that good? You never met her."

"Oh, I'm sure she was just fine," Mom says. "But it would be a shame, what with Emma's divorce and everything."

The room goes silent, as if no one is even breathing.

I'm incapable of hiding my reaction. I drop my fork and stare at her. "What did you say?"

Mom's forehead creases with concern. "I'm sorry, Hunter, I thought you knew. Emma Parker got divorced recently. I realize you two were an item a long time ago, but I thought..."

"You thought what?" I ask, my voice quiet. "That I'd give her a call and see if she wants to go out?"

"Well..."

"I appreciate the thought," I say. "But that was a long time ago."

Mom puts a hand over mine, but to my surprise, she doesn't say anything else about it.

We go back to our dinner, and it doesn't take long before the conversation picks up again—fortunately with topics that don't make us all squirm in our chairs. I try to focus on my dinner, but I barely taste it.

Emma Parker.

I loved Emma Parker from the first time I saw her. We were ten years old, and her family had just moved to Jetty Beach. The teacher put her at the desk right next to me. She had a thick blond ponytail tied with a pink ribbon.

I staunchly ignored her for the next six years, despite her attempts to be friendly. I had no idea what to do with my crush, so I harbored it secretly, never telling a soul. I didn't do the boy thing where I teased her as a sign of affection. I just avoided her. I think, even back then, I was afraid I'd screw things up. I was an angry kid, and I got in trouble a lot. Emma was quiet and sweet, and I couldn't imagine she'd want to be my friend, let alone my girlfriend.

By junior year, sports had given me a decent outlet for my pent-up rage, and I finally gathered enough courage to ask her out. I brought her to a movie, and spent half of it trying to work up the nerve to hold her hand. When I finally touched her, it was electric. We both gasped, staring straight ahead at the screen. Her fingers twined with mine and it was magic.

After that, we were inseparable. Emma was my first everything. First real date. First kiss. We lost our virginity together on a blow-up air mattress in the back of my old pickup truck. She was my first love.

My only love.

And yes, I'm the one who screwed it up.

I left to join the Marines, knowing it would hurt her. At the time, I thought it was my only choice. I wanted her to move on with her life—to find someone else and be happy.

When I came home a little more than a year ago, I found out she had indeed moved on. Hearing it was harder than I thought it would be. I didn't expect to find her still single and waiting for me—after all, I'd been gone nine years. But finding out she was married was devastating.

I had no right to be upset. I made the choice to leave. But it still hurt, hitting me in a place deep in my soul that I'd thought I had pretty well walled off.

So I put it behind me. As much as I wanted to make amends with Emma, coming back into her life would be cruel. I'd be doing it for me, not for her. She'd found happiness, and I wanted that for her more than anything else. I stayed away.

But now she's divorced?

I get through the meal without asking questions, but I'm

insane with curiosity. What happened? I don't know anything about the guy she married, and she doesn't live in town. I wonder how my mom knows. Is she hurt? Was it a mutual thing? Did she come back to Jetty Beach, or does she still live out in Cedar Hills?

After dessert, I make an excuse about needing to work early tomorrow, and head home. Maybe I should have just asked my mom what she knew, but it isn't my business. The fact that Emma's not married anymore doesn't change a thing. I still need to stay out of her life.

Don't I?

## 3

## EMMA

*L*oud music keeps me company on the drive out to Gabriel's, but it isn't enough. Even the highway is full of memories. You'd think that after a decade, it wouldn't bother me anymore. I pass the spot where my car broke down senior year, and my stomach turns. Hunter drove out in that old, broken-down truck of his, and picked me up. I drive by the turn to Forest Hill Road, the prime makeout spot for Jetty Beach teenagers, and I feel a little nauseated. I don't even want to think about what happened up there (spoiler: it was incredible).

The gateway sign proclaims *Welcome to Jetty Beach*, and I want to vomit. I hate that this place bothers me so much. I dated Hunter for two years—when I was a dumb teenager—and it's literally taken me longer to get over him than the jackass I actually married. I don't think there's a single place that would remind me of Wyatt enough to make me sad. Annoyed, maybe, that I wasted the better part of my twenties on him. But not sad.

I switch to another station playing this week's top twenty hits. Yes, modern music, from today. Nothing old. I'm starting new, and even though I've declared this year Project Get Emma Back, it's really a fresh start. I'm all about the new. About the now. Moving on.

Gabriel isn't home when I get there, so I let myself in. His house is such a bachelor pad, but I can't blame him. He got divorced too, a couple of years ago. I think he's still reeling over his wife leaving the way she did. If there's anyone in this world that pisses me off more than Wyatt, it's Amanda. That bitch broke my brother's heart into a thousand pieces, and she's lucky she ran off to Brazil or wherever she went. I'd really love to slap her. I'm all talk, I'd never be brave enough to actually do it. But I want to. Boy, do I want to.

Still, his place is comfortable, and of course it has a great kitchen. I think about taking him up on his offer to come up to the restaurant, but it's late, and he has a bunch of leftovers in his fridge. I fill up a plate and make myself at home on his couch, watching mindless reality shows while I wait for him to come home.

A couple hours later, the sound of the door opening jolts me awake. I must have fallen asleep. I smooth down my hair and try to act like I didn't just wake up.

"Hey, Emma," Gabe says.

I stand up to give him a hug. "Hey. How was work?"

"Busy," he says. "Did you get dinner?"

I smile. Of course his first concern is whether I've eaten. "Yeah, I raided your fridge."

"Good," he says. "So I'm stuck with you for how long?"

"About a week, I think. Maybe two."

He disappears into his bedroom for a minute, then comes out in a white t-shirt and sweats. "You need to move out of that place for good. Do you have a lease?"

"I'm month-to-month," I say. "And I know. But I can't

afford anything better."

"You should just move here for now."

"Here?" I ask. "Like, Jetty Beach?"

"No, I mean here," he says, pointing downward. "My place. I have an extra room. You should have moved here to begin with. Just for a while, until you get back on your feet. That apartment is a piece of shit."

My shoulders tighten. "I know it's a piece of shit, but I'm on my feet. I have a job. I can take care of myself."

"Of course you can, Emma. That's not what I meant. All I'm saying is, I have three bedrooms, and I'm practically never here. There's no reason for you to live in some dump."

He's right; it does make sense for me to room with him for a while. He was baffled when I didn't last year, when I left Wyatt. I couldn't bring myself to tell him why. He'd think I was a pathetic idiot. Who cares what happened ten years ago? Why should that still bother me? His wife left him— and I know that was awful—and he still lives in the house they shared.

What does it say about me, that I feel the need to swear off an entire town because my high school boyfriend left me?

"You know what, you're right," I say. "I will. I'll get my stuff out of there when they finish poisoning the place to kill the bugs."

He laughs, and I take a seat on a barstool.

"Does Mom know you're in town?" he asks.

"Not yet."

"Are you going to go see her?" he asks.

"At some point, yeah. Will you come with me?"

He gives me a sidelong glance. "Do I have to?"

"Come on, let's go tomorrow and get it over with," I say.

He groans. "Do you know what happened last time I

visited Mom? She tried to set me up with someone."

It's my turn to groan. "Who?"

"I don't know, I didn't let her get that far," he says. "Just you wait. She'll be on to you next."

"Oh, hell no," I say. "That is the absolute last thing I need. Don't you think she'll give me a grace period or something? My divorce was just finalized."

"Do you know our mother?" he asks. "She probably has a list already."

I shake my head. "No way. Not gonna happen. I am not dating anyone. Maybe ever."

Gabe pulls out a bottle of Jameson and two glasses. "I think we need to drink to that."

"To what?" I ask.

"To not dating," he says.

"I can absolutely drink to that."

"To staying single," he says.

"Fuck relationships," I say.

He smiles and we both drink.

"Fuck relationships indeed," he says. "Want another?"

Warmth spreads through my belly. "You know what? I'll have one more."

"Sounds good," Gabe says.

He pours another and I toss it back. It's pleasant. I feel lighter than I have in a while.

"So I assume you have to work tomorrow," I say.

"It's Saturday," he says. "Of course I do." He drinks his second shot. "Not until about noon, though. I'm going down to the farmers' market in the morning. There's a grower I want to talk to. Want to come along?"

I suppose I can't sit around Gabe's place all day, and the farmers' market is pretty innocuous as far as memories go. "Sure."

"Great," he says. "Get up early, though. I want to be there when they open at nine."

We hang out for a while, catching up on life. I feel guilty for not spending more time with my brother, especially because he's alone now. I've let this place get to me way more than it should. It's just a town.

And it isn't like Hunter is even *here*. He's been gone for ten years. The worst I'll run into are reminders of him, and I can certainly handle that. Maybe what I need is some exposure therapy. I'll spend some time in town, and maybe Jetty Beach won't seem like such a hotbed of bad memories. Maybe I can finally be free of its spell.

And of him.

THE FARMERS' market is charming. It's held in a wide open field just outside downtown, with rows of white canopies displaying food, crafts, art—all sorts of things. It's grown a lot since I was a kid, when it was just a handful of vendors selling produce. Gabe finds the grower he wants to talk to, and I wait nearby. The sun is warm already, although a light breeze is blowing in off the water. It's going to be a gorgeous day. The market fills quickly as people wander in from the parking area, and the hum of conversation fills the air.

Gabe hands me a few strawberries to sample. They're shiny red, and I pop one in my mouth as I wander down the path. The flavor explodes in my mouth. I almost forgot how amazing fresh, organic strawberries are. I eat another one and glance at a booth selling beaded jewelry. Gabe is still chatting with the grower, so I move on down the line.

I stop outside another booth, this one full of huge bouquets wrapped in thick white paper. The fragrance of fresh cut flowers spills across the walkway. I pick up a bouquet and take a big whiff. It smells heavenly.

"How much?" I ask.

The woman running the booth answers. "Ten dollars for the large ones, five for the small. You can choose one that's already put together, or we can custom make something for you."

I pull out a five-dollar bill and hand it to her, and pick one of the smaller bouquets. I'm thinking that Gabe needs a little feminine touch in his house—and then my back prickles, and I have the distinct feeling that someone is watching me. I glance behind me, half afraid I'm going to see Wyatt. He can't be here. He knows where my family lives, but would he come out here looking for me? Is he actually following me, or am I just being paranoid? I see Gabe still chatting with the grower, but no sign of Wyatt. I smile at the vendor and grab my flowers, breathing out a long breath. I'm definitely being paranoid.

I notice someone out of the corner of my eye, and I swear he's looking right at me. I look up, but he's already turned around, walking away through the crowd.

My stomach does a flip. It can't be.

I put a hand to my forehead, angry with myself for being so stupid. I'm trying to get over my feelings about this place, and here I am, seeing things. Believing I see Hunter in the crowd is worse than imagining Wyatt following me around. Hunter is gone. He left ten years ago. I don't like to think about it, but I have to be honest with myself—I don't even know if he's still alive. He was in the Marines, after all. He's probably a million miles away, all thoughts of me long forgotten.

I wish I could forget him, too.

## 4

# HUNTER

*I* pull my truck into the parking spot at the farmers' market. It just opened, but already the walkways are full of people. The sun is out, there isn't a cloud in the sky, and it looks like every person in Jetty Beach is here. Crowds are not my favorite thing, but I'm only here to help Ryan pick up a bench for our mom. I'll be in and out in no time.

I spot Ryan near the entrance, talking to Nicole. He kisses her, and I decide to wait rather than approach. I put my hands in my pockets and glance away.

*Get on with it, Ryan, for the love—*

Nicole pulls away and smiles, then walks into the market.

"You guys need to get a fucking room," I say as I walk toward Ryan.

"Whatever, dick," he says, but he smiles.

"So what are we doing here, again?" I ask, dropping the subject. I might give Ryan a lot of shit, but I actually love seeing him happy.

"Mom bought a bench, I guess?" He says it like he's not

quite sure either. "She said it should be near the entrance, so maybe it's that one over there."

He points to a booth with handmade furniture and wooden decor. It looks like the right sort of place, so we find the craftsman. The bench, a simple design with dark wood slats, is just inside the booth. It's beautiful and a little bit rustic, which is perfect for Mom.

I go around to one side and Ryan takes the other. I look up into the crowd and feel a mild tug of surprise. Gabriel Parker, Emma's brother, is standing not far down the row of canopies, talking with someone in front of a large booth of fruits and vegetables.

I'm used to seeing Gabriel around. He lives and works in Jetty Beach. In fact, Cody's fiancée Clover works for him at his restaurant. I see him around town occasionally, but he doesn't take notice of me. Truth be told, he probably doesn't know who I am. He's older than Emma by several years, and he lived in Europe the whole time I dated his sister—not to mention when I left her.

He probably doesn't know I exist, which is fine. It's bad enough I have to worry about running into her mom, who I would imagine remembers me all too well. So far, that hasn't happened though.

"Here, you get this end," Ryan says.

I pick up the other side of the bench—*fuck, why did she have to pick the heaviest one here?*—and almost drop it.

Gabriel isn't alone.

I see her from the back, and instantly I know it's her. I don't even have to see her face. Her hair is up in a ponytail, long strands of blond hair hanging down to her shoulders. She's wearing a purple tank top and a pair of shorts, and her body is everything I remember: narrow waist, toned arms, strong legs.

She turns, and my heart nearly beats out of my chest. Ten years, and she's hardly changed. She's still the most beautiful woman I've ever laid eyes on.

"Dude, Hunter," Ryan says.

I adjust my grip on the bench. "Sorry."

I look for her again, but she's not there. Shit. I can't keep standing in one place, staring, holding this stupid bench. So I walk out toward my truck, holding up my end. Ryan and I move it across the grass to the parking lot and get it in the back, where I secure it with a strap so it won't slide around, then close the tailgate.

"You got this?" Ryan asks. "Your leg okay?"

I'm so distracted, looking toward the market, I almost don't hear him. "Yeah, I got it. I'm fine. Dad can help me unload it when I get to their place."

"Okay, sounds good," he says. "I'm going to go track down Nicole."

I nod, but I'm barely listening. Was it really her?

I have to find out.

Feeling like I should be armed and wearing body armor, I slip back into the crowded market. More people are pouring in from the parking area. I find a spot where no one will walk behind me—I have issues with people being behind me if I'm standing in one place—and narrow my eyes, trying to spot her. Or her brother.

My eyes comb the crowd, moving quickly from face to face. She could be anywhere, or she could have left already. There's a steady stream of people walking up and down the walkway between the booths.

I'm just about to give up and take the bench to my mom's house when I catch sight of her. She's farther down the line of canopies, smelling a bouquet of flowers. I take an involuntary step closer. My heart thunders in my chest. It's been so long.

Fuck, she's so beautiful it's insane. Delicate chin, sweet little turned-up nose. She smiles at the vendor.

Damn it. Why did I ever leave her? People say eighteen-year-old boys are idiots, but in my case that's the understatement of the century. Did I really leave that behind? There's something different about her now. Her hips are a little curvier, her breasts a little fuller. When I left, she was still a girl.

She's a woman now.

My dick twitches to life and my heart starts racing. Her face lifts, and I turn away in a panic. A jolt of adrenaline courses through me and my back clenches.

The crowd is too close. There's a burning sensation in my chest and I can't quite catch my breath. *Fuck.* I definitely have to get out of here.

I walk back to the edge of the market, forcing myself to take careful steps. I want to sprint, but I know my leg won't let me; trying to run hurts, and pain will only make my panic worse. I can usually handle crowds, but seeing Emma sent such a huge spike of adrenaline through my system that I'm dangerously close to having an attack. My rational brain knows I'm not in danger, but my primal brain doesn't listen. My body reacts differently now.

I get in my truck and take a deep breath. *I'm home. I'm not in danger. It's okay that I'm not armed.*

My hands grip the steering wheel and I slow my breathing. In and out, repeating my mantras. *I'm home. I'm not in danger. I'm home. I'm not in danger.*

*I'm home.*

By the time I reach my parent's place, my heart rate is normal and I'm pretty sure I'll be able to talk without rousing suspicion. My mom is a worrier, and I don't want to give her more reasons to be concerned about me. I drop off the bench, helping Dad place it on the back porch where Mom wants it. They ask if I'd like to stay, but I let them know I have somewhere to be.

I have a date.

I DRIVE the forty-five minutes out to Sequoia Ridge. I go most Saturdays, as long as work doesn't interfere. The curtain parts at the front window as soon as I pull up to the house, and I can't help but smile.

Before I even get out of my truck, Isaac runs out the front door. His brown hair flops around on top of his head and his face lights up with a smile. His Spiderman t-shirt has a red stain near the collar, but somehow being dirty just makes the kid look cuter.

"Uncle Hunter!"

I crouch down and he runs into my arms. I wrap him in a big hug, feeling his little arms coil around my neck.

"Hi, buddy," I say.

He squeezes me tighter. I stand up, still holding on to him, and carry him inside.

Isaac is five, and although he calls me Uncle Hunter, we aren't related. For a guy like me, family titles have almost nothing to do with blood, so I'm proud to be his uncle.

I hug him again and set him down. "Where's Grandma?"

"Upstairs," he says. "She'll be down in a minute. Do I get to come to your house?"

"I'm sorry, bud, I can't take you home with me this time." My chest clenches at the disappointment in his face. "Maybe next time, okay?"

Elaine's voice breaks in. "I thought I heard you come in."

I look up and see her coming down the stairs. She's walking slow, holding onto the railing. I was hoping she'd look better than the last time I saw her, but she doesn't. If anything, she looks worse.

"Hi, Elaine," I say. "How are you feeling?"

She gets to the bottom of the stairs and waves a hand. "Oh, I'm doing just fine."

I know she's lying, but she doesn't want to say anything in front of Isaac. I'm not even sure if I know about all Elaine's ailments. The ones she's admitted to are bad enough: arthritis, a clotting disorder that makes bleeding dangerous, and something that gives her poor immune system function. She gets sick a lot.

Elaine's son, Major Anthony Lynch, was one of my closest friends in the Corps. His girlfriend, Mary, died when Isaac was born, and Elaine took care of Isaac during Anthony's deployments. Unfortunately, when Anthony and I were overseas, he drove over an IED. He didn't come home.

"Uncle Hunter, look," Isaac says, holding up a Spiderman action figure.

"Wow, buddy, look at that," I say. "Is that new?"

"Yeah, Grandma got it for me."

"That's awesome. Spiderman is your thing now, huh?"

"Yeah," he says. "He shoots webs."

"He sure does," I say. "So, what do you want to do today?"

"I want to go to the park, and get ice cream, and play, and watch a movie, and—"

"Okay, okay, I get it," I say with a laugh. "We probably don't have time for all that, but I think we can start with the park and go from there."

"Go get your shoes on," Elaine says.

Isaac bounds up the stairs, sounding like a herd of elephants instead of a fifty-pound little boy.

I lower my voice. "How are you, really?"

Elaine sighs. "It could be worse. My doctor has me on new medication and it seems to be helping."

"Good," I say. I pull a check, already made out and signed, out of my pocket and press it into her hand.

"Hunter, you don't have to do this," Elaine says.

"I know," I say. "It isn't about *have to*."

"I always use it for Isaac," she says.

"Use it for whatever you need," I say. "And if you ever need anything else, I want you to call me, okay?"

Elaine presses her lips together and nods.

Isaac runs down the stairs, making more noise than he did on the way up. "Let's go," he says.

I brush the hair off his forehead. "You need a haircut. Maybe we'll do that too." I look up at Elaine. "I'll have him home in time for bed."

"You two boys have a good time," she says.

"We will," Isaac says, already halfway out the door.

I watch Isaac skip down the path to my truck, his hair flying with each bounce. I made a promise to his father that if anything ever happened to him, I'd look out for his son. As soon as I got home, I got in touch with Elaine. As someone who lost both my parents, I felt terrible for the poor kid. I knew he'd need a man in his life, and Elaine lives close enough that I can drive to see them, so I make it a point to do so as often as possible.

At first Isaac wasn't too sure about me. He wanted his daddy, and I certainly couldn't blame him. But after a couple months, he warmed up to me; now he and I are good buddies. I look forward to my visits with him. I wish I could do more.

Elaine waves at me from her front porch. I'm worried about her ability to continue to care for Isaac. She's nearing seventy, and her health has been declining pretty rapidly since I've known them. Her husband died a few years ago, and I know she struggles to take care of her grandson. I'm worried about what's going to happen to Isaac if Elaine can't keep him. He doesn't have anyone else.

He's so much like me.

I spend the afternoon with Isaac. We hang out at a local playground, and I take him to get a haircut. Afterward, we get ice cream—and I realize too late that I probably should have fed him dinner first. I get him some fast food before taking him home, making sure we're back in time so he can take a bath. He's pretty filthy. That tends to happen when I'm with him. He's a rough and tumble kid with a lot of energy, so I do my best to wear him out.

Of course, I'm the one worn out by the end of our visits.

After his bath, he comes down in a fresh pair of Spiderman pajamas. I take him upstairs, tuck him in, and kiss him on the head.

Elaine is sitting on the couch when I leave. I make sure she doesn't get up. I say goodbye, and head home. I'm dead tired, but I feel content on the drive. Spending time with Isaac is always good for me.

I roll down the window for the fresh air, and my thoughts drift back to Emma. I kept her on the outskirts of my mind all afternoon, but now that I'm alone, I can't stop thinking about her.

My reaction to seeing her was so intense. I've wondered for years what it would be like to see her again, but I wasn't prepared for such a surge. It isn't just her beauty—although she's every bit as gorgeous as I remember. She opened up a place inside that I buried years ago. A place I didn't think was accessible anymore.

Maybe I should have called her after I came home last year, at least to explain. I owe her that much. Hell, I owe her more than I could ever give, and that's part of what's kept me away. I didn't want to intrude on her life, but I also know I betrayed her in a way she might never be able to forgive. And if she couldn't, it would be devastating all over again.

But now that I've seen her, I know.

I have to talk to her. Even if it fails miserably, I have to take that chance.

I can't stay away from her.

## 5

## HUNTER

*K*nowing I want to see Emma, and actually making it happen, are two different things.

Sunday morning, I walk out on my back porch with a cup of coffee. I'm not sure what I'll say to her when I do see her, but the first step is finding her. I need to make contact. The problem is, I'm not sure how.

I go back inside, grab a spiral notebook, and sit down. My instincts take over, and I make a list of my assets, as if Emma is a mission.

Truck, for transportation.

Internet, for research.

Visual sighting in town.

I tap the ball point pen against the coffee table. That's not much to work with. In fact, it's essentially nothing, because I don't know where she lives or how to contact her. She was with Gabriel, so that's something. I know where he works, but that doesn't do me a whole lot of good. It isn't like I can show up at his restaurant and ask about her. He doesn't know who the fuck I am—which, to be fair, is a point in my favor.

Nevertheless, I don't think me approaching Gabriel is a good plan, but I do know someone who knows him. Clover works for him. Maybe she'll know something about Emma, like whether she's staying with her brother or just in town for a visit.

I text Clover to see if she's around. She says she has to head into work in a couple of hours, but she can meet me for coffee.

I pull up to Old Town Cafe. It's busy inside, a long line of people stretching back from the counter. That's Jetty Beach during the summer for you, particularly when the sun comes out. Clover isn't here yet, so I order coffee for both of us and find a small table near the back.

Clover comes in, beaming that huge smile at me. Despite how anxious I'm feeling, I can't help but smile back. It's hard not to. Clover is the happiest person on the planet. It's pretty infectious.

"Hey, almost-brother," she says. She scrunches up her shoulders and her blond curls bounce around her face. "I love calling you that."

"Whatever makes you happy, weirdo," I say with a wink. I actually like it when she calls me that, too.

"So, what's up?" she asks. "Cody was trying so hard to play it cool, like he's not insanely curious why you need to talk to me, but I made him stay home."

"Thanks for that," I say. "I don't know if I want to talk to him about this right now."

"I know," she says, with a solemn nod of her head. "I could tell."

"From my text?" I ask, drawing my eyebrows together.

"I'm very perceptive," she says. "What's going on? Is this about Emma?"

I take a deep breath. "Yes, it's about Emma."

"Thought so," she says. "Ever since your mom mentioned her at dinner the other night, I've been wondering when I'd hear this story. Cody wouldn't tell me, other than you guys dated a long time ago."

"There's not much to tell," I say. Or rather, there's not much I'm going to tell Clover. She doesn't need all the gory details. "Emma and I were together in high school. After graduation, I left to join the Marines. I don't really want to get into why, but I was gone a long time, and she moved on. Except, as my mom blurted out at dinner, she's apparently divorced. I was okay with that. But then I saw her yesterday."

Clover tilts her head and clasps her hands together. "Aw, that is so sweet. Was she happy to see you?"

"No, she didn't see me," I say. "I saw her at the market. But I left before I had a chance to talk to her."

"And then what?" she asks, leaning forward.

"No, that's all," I say. "I saw her and I want to talk to her. But I don't know where she lives, or how to get hold of her."

"You're such a guy," she says.

"What was I supposed to do?" I ask. "I haven't seen her in a decade, and honestly, I don't think she's going to want to see me."

"So what do you need me for?"

"Like I said, I don't know where she lives or how to get in touch," I say. "But you know someone who does."

"I do?"

"She's Gabriel Parker's sister."

"Gabriel?" Clover says, her voice a little squeal. "No way. Your ex-girlfriend is my boss's sister? How is that even possible?"

"It's a small town," I say with a shrug.

"Okay, so what do you want me to do?" She looks way too excited about this.

"Honestly, I'm not sure," I say. "Has Gabriel said anything about his sister being in town?"

She shakes her head. "No, but we don't talk about anything other than work. He's not very chatty when it comes to his life outside the kitchen. I didn't even know he had a sister."

I sit back in my seat. Shit. This isn't helping, and now that Clover knows, it's only a matter of time before Cody does. Word is going to get back to my mom, and then I'm in trouble. My mom is not known for keeping out of things, whether or not they're her business.

"That sucks," I say. "I could probably find out where Gabriel lives, but that's treading into creepy stalker territory."

Clover's eyes go wide and she smiles, her white teeth practically gleaming. "That's totally what we should do."

"What?"

"Be creepy stalkers!"

Oh, shit. "What are you talking about?"

"Come on, you were in the military and stuff. You must know how to do this kind of thing, right? Except we're not finding bad guys, we're finding the love of your life."

"Okay, slow down there, slick," I say. "First of all, I don't think stalking my ex-girlfriend is a great way to start an apology. And second, I never said she was the love of my life."

"Whatever, she totally is," she says with a wave of her hand. "What kind of cool equipment do you have? Do you have night vision goggles? Oh my god, I've always wanted to use night vision goggles. Can I try them?"

My mouth opens, but I just stare at her. I actually do have night vision goggles, but I probably shouldn't tell her that. "I don't think we need night vision goggles."

"Fine." She takes a sip of coffee and scrunches up her face, looking up at the ceiling like she's thinking really hard.

I'm starting to wonder if telling Clover was a good idea.

"I know what to do," she blurts out. "Okay, my job will be to find out what I can about Emma, and find out where Gabriel lives. I'm pretty sure I can get into his office at work and find something we can work with."

"Clover, no," I say. "Do not break into your boss's office."

"Why?" she asks. "He won't know. I'll be like a ninja."

I raise an eyebrow. "You are not like a ninja."

"Don't worry about it," she says, getting up. "I'll do my part and report back at oh-eight-hundred-hours."

I start laughing and almost choke. "Are you serious?"

"I've always wanted to say that," she says, then turns and flits out of the cafe before I can stop her.

I have a bad feeling about this.

HOW THE FUCK did I end up here?

I glance over at Clover. She's dressed in a dark green t-shirt and pair of camo shorts, and her hair is pulled up. She smiles at me and hunkers further down in the ditch.

Yes, I'm in a ditch.

Across from Gabriel's house.

This is the literal worst.

"Clover, this is a really bad idea."

"Shh," she says, putting a finger to her lips.

She did in fact text me at eight, giving me a set of cross streets with the word "coordinates." Curiosity got the better of my judgment. I picked her up and parked up the road from where I'm currently sitting. She had a look of triumph on her face when she declared she'd not only figured out where Gabriel lives, she found out Emma is in fact staying with him, and she drives a blue Toyota Corolla.

Then she somehow talked me into hiding in a ditch across from his house, waiting to see if Emma comes out.

"What am I supposed to do if she comes out?" I say, gazing at the blue car in the driveway. Is that really hers? It looks like something she would drive. Small and practical, but still cute. It's at least a few years old, and I wonder if she's been getting the oil changed regularly.

"Go talk to her."

"What?" I ask. "I should just pop out of the ditch and say hello?"

"Okay, follow her, then," Clover says.

"We really don't need to sit out here," I say. "Now that I know where she is, I can come over and knock on the door like a normal person."

"Will you?" Clover says, arching an eyebrow at me.

I don't answer.

"See," she says. "You need motivation. You saw her once, and it was enough to get you to bring me in on this. You need to see her again. I bet she walks out that door and you can't help yourself. You'll go for it this time."

"Clover, you are completely insane. I—"

I stop talking, my thought completely gone. Emma just walked out the front door.

My heart starts beating too fast again, and I take a few deep breaths. She's dressed in jeans and a white t-shirt, with her hair down and blue sandals on her feet. I'm mesmerized. I almost could have convinced myself I imagined her at the market on Saturday, but now that I see her again, she's so real.

Emma pauses at her driver's side door and looks around.

I duck behind the embankment. *Oh god, please don't look over here. Please don't look.*

Clover has a hand clamped to her mouth, and her eyes are wide. I shake my head at her and mouth a very emphatic *No*.

The car starts up, and a few seconds later Emma drives away.

"Go!" Clover says. "Get to the truck!"

We dash down the road to the empty lot where I parked my truck, and take off after her. I have no idea what I'm doing, but I feel like I can't let her get away. The rational part of my brain is trying to remind me that I know where to find her now. I don't have to follow her like some psycho. But I catch a glimpse of blue bumper, Clover shrieks and points it out, and I keep driving.

I hang back, keeping my distance, my heart racing. This is so stupid. What am I supposed to do when she stops? What if she leaves town and gets on the highway? I can't keep following her, but the thought of missing my chance to talk to her makes my stomach turn.

Relief washes over me when she turns into Charlie's Grocery. I see her pull into a parking spot, so I circle around the block. I don't want to follow her in. I feel like such a creeper already.

"Go back," Clover says. "What are you doing?"

"What am I supposed to do?"

"Go to the grocery store, obviously," she says. "This is perfect. You can wait for her to come out and pretend it's all a big coincidence."

"And what, spill my guts to her outside her car?"

"I don't know," Clover says. "Maybe invite her to coffee or something."

I shake my head. "She won't do it."

"You know this?"

"Would you?" I ask. "If you saw the man who left you ten years ago, and he appears out of nowhere in a fucking parking lot, would you be happy to see him and go grab some coffee?"

She pauses, like she has to think about that one.

"See?" I ask.

"Well, we did not go to all this trouble for you to drive around like a big baby," she says. "Go back to the store, and wait for her. I'll wait in the truck while you get out and talk to her. It'll be fine."

I take a deep breath and pull into the grocery store parking lot, just across from where her car is parked. I turn so I can see the front door, and wait.

## 6

# EMMA

*I*'m incapable of not overbuying at the grocery store. I was supposed to grab a few staples so I'd have more than Gabriel's leftovers to eat when he's at work, but apparently that meant a cart full of stuff. I push it out to my car and start unloading everything into the trunk.

My back prickles again, like someone is looking at me. It makes my shoulders clench. I put another bag in the trunk, telling myself I'm being paranoid. I haven't seen Wyatt in months. I need to stop worrying that he's following me around.

Of course, he did follow me around for the first six months after I left him, so I suppose my concern is justified. But he's not here. He can't be here.

The feeling doesn't go away. I keep unloading my groceries, and finally decide the best thing to do is look. It's probably just a seagull staring at me or something. I'll see that no one's there, and I can stop worrying about it.

I glance over my shoulder, and my heart feels like it's literally in my throat.

It can't be.

I blink hard, sure I'm seeing things. It's like the market yesterday. I'm so anxious about being in Jetty Beach, about facing all the memories of the two of us here, that it's making me hallucinate. Hunter is not standing next to a green pickup truck, looking at me. He's not.

I blink again. He's just as tall as I remember, but thicker —broad chest, arms bulging with muscle. His hair is shorter, and he looks older. He's no longer a boy; he looks like a man—a big, strong, beautiful man ... and my body is utterly betraying me, turning my knees to Jell-O at the sight of him. His eyes are fixed on me, his expression unreadable. He's totally unmoving, like he's as frozen as I feel, like we're both caught in some sort of time vortex, hovering between this moment and ten years ago.

He takes a deep breath, his chest rising and falling against his black t-shirt. When did he get those tattoos on his arms? He walks toward me and I can't move. I can't breathe. Can't think.

This can't be Hunter. This can't be real.

"Emma," he says.

That voice. Oh my god, he sounds like Hunter, only better. Deeper. Rougher.

I swallow hard, trying to think of something to say, but all I can do is stare.

He stops a few feet from me and rubs the back of his neck. "I, um. I'm sorry to surprise you like this."

Wait, did he just use the word *sorry*? Hunter Evans, the man who ripped my heart to pieces and threw it in the fucking trash? Oh, he is not sorry. But he's going to be.

Anger floods through me, breaking me out of my stupor. I slam the trunk closed and he blinks, taking a step back.

"Are you serious?" I ask. Even I'm surprised at the venom in my voice. I'm not usually so aggressive.

"I..." He stammers a little, not quite getting anything coherent out.

"What the hell?" I say. "I haven't seen you in ten fucking years, and you're going to just walk up to me in a parking lot and say hi?"

"Emma, you have every right to be mad—"

"You bet I do." I'm on a roll now, and he's not stopping me. I've been waiting ten years to unload on this asshole. "I'm not just mad, Hunter. I'm livid. Yes, even after all these years, and I don't care what kind of pathetic loser that makes me. You left, in the middle of the fucking night, without a word. And then nothing. I hear nothing from you. Do you have any idea what kind of a hell that was?"

He shakes his head. "No, I don't."

"Well, I'll tell you," I say. "It was the worst experience of my entire life—and after the year I've had, that's saying something. You do not have the right to walk up to me like some old friend." Tears are threatening to fall, but I don't want to cry in front of him. I don't want to cry at all. I thought I used up all the tears I had for him a long time ago.

His brow furrows, and his eyes show so much pain. I should not care that he looks sad. I should *want* to hurt him. Seeing him makes me feel like a teenager all over again, a little girl with a broken heart. I imagined this moment a thousand times over the years, and none of them involved him looking at me like that. So sad. So sorry.

No. I'm not letting him get away with it.

"Fuck you, Hunter," I say. I'm losing it and I know I should get out of here. I go to my driver's side door, abandoning the cart where it sits.

"Emma," he says.

I stop.

*Open the door, Emma. Open the door, get in, and drive away. Don't listen to him.*

"Emma, please," he says. "I have no right to ask for your forgiveness. That isn't why I'm here."

"Then what do you want?"

"I ... fuck, I don't know," he says. "I saw you the other day and it was like getting hit by a train. After I got back, I left you alone. I didn't want to interfere, but then I saw you and—"

"Wait, when did you get back?" I ask.

"Last year," he says. "March, I guess."

More than a year ago? He's been home that long? The desire to know what happened to him wars with my desire to still be mad. A million questions run through my mind. Why did he come home? Where does he live now? Is he married? Kids? What has he done with the last ten years of his life?

Why did he leave me in the first place?

"Look, maybe we could go somewhere and talk?" he asks.

"How did you even find me here?" I ask.

Surprise crosses his face. "Um," he says, rubbing the back of his neck again. He pauses before answering. "I actually followed you."

"From where?"

"Your brother's house."

A fresh wave of anger pours through me. "What?"

"I know," he says. "That sounds really bad. I didn't mean ... fuck ... I don't know how to explain this."

A woman gets out of his truck, and my mouth drops open. She's petite, and way too fucking cute for me to deal with right now, with curly blond hair, and a pair of very tiny camo shorts showing off an amazing set of legs. She has a big rock on her left hand. Is this his wife? What the fuck?

She stands next to Hunter and grabs his arm, bouncing up and down onto her tip toes. "Hi," she says, holding out her hand, and flashes me a wide smile. "I'm Clover."

I'm completely speechless.

Her face falls a little and she lets her hand drop.

"Clover, I don't think now is the time," Hunter says.

My eyes move from Hunter to Clover. Is that seriously her name? My chest feels like it's going to cave in. I shouldn't care that he's married. I was married. Why can't he have found someone?

But if he's married to *this*, why is he standing in a parking lot trying to talk to me like it matters what happened between us a decade ago?

"I'm sorry, did I ruin things?" Clover asks. "She looked really mad and I thought you could use a little help."

"What the hell?" I ask.

"Hunter just really wanted to talk to you," Clover says. "It's my fault he followed you here. That was my idea."

"Okay, Clover, maybe that's enough helping for today," Hunter says.

"Sorry, Emma," Clover says. "It was really nice to meet you." She turns to Hunter and whispers loudly. "I'll bounce. Cody can come get me over at Old Town. I'll walk."

She gives me a cheerful wave and starts walking toward downtown.

I gape at Hunter. "Why? Who?"

He looks between me and Clover. "Her?" His eyes widen and he holds up a hand. "Oh, my god, no. No, she's Cody's fiancée. Shit, that probably looked like—no. No, Clover was just trying to help me out, in her own weird way. She works for your brother, so she found out where he lives. And like an idiot I let her talk me into following you."

The relief I feel makes me want to cry again. He's not married? I try to focus on his hands without making it obvious I'm looking for a ring. No ring. Just those calloused hands with thick fingers, his strong forearms, and those tattoos...

*Stop it, Emma. You're mad at this man. Furious.*

"This is not going well," Hunter says. "Emma, I've done a lot of things I'm not proud of, and I carry a lot of regrets. Like I said, I'm not here expecting you to forgive me. But I hoped you might be willing to talk. Even just catch up. Not a day has gone by in the last ten years that I haven't thought about you. I know I have no right to ask anything of you, but can we talk?"

I feel like I'm sinking. After all this time, is Hunter really standing in front of me? If I let him go now, I might never see him again. I want to stay angry, but should I walk away from this chance? How often have I dreamt of this moment?

I want answers. I want to know why. Maybe if he explains to me why he left, I can finally be free of him.

No. I can't give him any more of my time. I'll be free of him because I *choose* to be. He had his chance years ago, and what he did left scars that will never fully heal. *Why* doesn't matter. It won't change anything. Nothing can change the past.

"No," I say, shaking my head. "No, we can't talk."

I turn away from his face. I can't see that expression, the one that looks like I just slapped him. Maybe hitting him would give me some closure, but I don't do it. I know I can't touch him or I'll melt into a big puddle in the middle of the parking lot, and I won't have the strength to refuse him.

I get in my car, turn it on, and drive away as fast as I can.

## 7

# HUNTER

*I* stare at Emma's car as she drives away. I already memorized the license plate. That probably makes me a bad person, and I didn't really mean to. The thought went through my mind that it would be good intel, and before I could stop myself, it was burned in my memory.

That doesn't mean I have to do anything with it. She made it pretty clear how she feels. She wants nothing to do with me.

I straighten, taking another deep breath to clear my head. No. That is not how this ends. Seeing her face, hearing her voice ... it was magic. *She's* magic. She always has been, and I let her go once. I'm not going to let her go again.

Granted, I have to get her back first.

Cody pulls up, with Clover in the passenger seat. He leans out his window, and I realize I'm still standing in the middle of the parking lot, staring up the street at a car that's been gone for at least two minutes.

"You okay?" he asks.

"Yeah, I'm fine."

"Did you really see Emma?"

"Yeah."

"What happened?"

I tear my eyes away from the street. "She left. She didn't want to talk to me."

"Ouch," Cody says. "Sorry, man."

"It's okay," I say, and I mean it. "I just realized something."

"What's that?"

"I'm going to marry Emma Parker."

Cody gapes at me, but I'm not worried about him right now. I know, in that deep place in my soul where Emma has always lived, that she's going to be mine. She doesn't know it yet, and I'm going to have to work my ass off to regain her trust. But even if it takes another ten years, I will. I'll prove to her that she can trust me again. She can love me the way I love her.

Because holy shit, if seeing her again proved anything to me, it's that I never, ever stopped loving her.

MAYBE I SHOULDN'T APPROACH Emma as a mission, but it's how my brain works. It's a pleasant afternoon, so I sit out on my back porch, spiral notebook in hand. It will be a multi-phase operation, and I write down some notes.

*Phase one: reconnaissance.* Clover already took care of most of that, but I should probably pump my mom for some more information. I don't like going in blind, and details could help me avoid surprises.

*Phase two: initial contact.* Today was a botched attempt at phase two, which is why I have to proceed with caution before I try again. Success will be measured by acceptance of an offer for coffee together. I'll need to make it hard for her to refuse, or at least easy to accept.

*Phase three: building trust.* This could be a long phase, and I'll probably need to divide it into sub-phases. I'm not starting at zero here, I'm starting at about negative fifty. Success will be measured by acceptance of an escalating series of dates. I'll start with coffee—the transition from phase two to three. That's not too much of a commitment. Once we have coffee—as many times as it takes for her to feel comfortable—I'll try for something more serious and date-like. Dinner, with me picking her up at her place. Until then, I'll plan to meet her at neutral locations.

*Phase four: official relationship.* Success will be measured by her willingness to refer to me as her boyfriend. This phase feels particularly tenuous, because it's entirely in her hands. I can't push for phase four too hard, and defining it will depend on a lot of factors that are outside my control.

*Phase five: engagement and marriage.* Success will be defined by an accepted proposal. Phase five seems a long way off, given how she looked like she might hit me earlier today. But the mission parameters should always be defined ahead of time. And that's the goal. That's where this ends. There's no question in my mind.

I sit back and look at my outline. There are a lot of variables I can't account for, the biggest one being the fact that Emma hates me. It's a tall order, going from hate to happily ever after, but I've faced worse odds. It isn't like she's literally trying to kill me.

I imagine her in those shorts, her hair falling down around her shoulders. I didn't put sex in the mission outline. I'm honestly not sure where it falls. I'm a guy, I could insert it anywhere. If she walked up to my door right now and wanted an angry fuck, I don't think I'd be able to say no. But that isn't Emma, and being intimate with her physically is going to take a lot of trust building. As badly as I want to feel her body against me, this won't be something I can rush. I'll have to be patient, and let her take the lead.

But when she's ready ... I'm going to do things to her she's never dreamed. She was my first, and I'm not even bragging when I say I wasn't bad back then. But now? No contest.

My gut tells me I need to give her a little space before I make another attempt at phase two. She probably remembers me as a hot-headed kid, but I've mellowed since then. I learned a lot about patience in the Marines. I know she needs me to be patient now, and will for the foreseeable future. That won't be a problem.

I've made a lot of mistakes in my life, but losing Emma Parker forever will not be one of them.

## 8

## EMMA

*A*fter seeing Hunter, I don't even know what to do with myself. I go back to Gabe's place in a daze. I put away the groceries, going through the motions, but I can't focus on what I'm doing. I wind up putting ice cream in the pantry and a can of soup in the freezer, but I figure out my mistake before I make too much of a mess.

My anger dissipates, leaving me feeling hollow. Hunter is home. He's here in Jetty Beach, and he followed me to the store so he could talk to me. Either I'm really losing it, and I imagined the whole thing, or that just happened.

I pop the cork on a bottle of Salishan Cellars Cabernet, realizing after I've poured a glass that it's still morning. I decide I don't care, and stand in the kitchen, sipping wine, trying to get my bearings.

Did I do the right thing by walking away? Would it have been better if I'd agreed to talk to him?

I honestly have no idea. Seeing him left me so off kilter that I'm not sure which way is up.

I'm distracted for the rest of the day, but I don't tell Gabe I saw Hunter. He doesn't really know about Hunter—he lived in Europe when I was in high school, so he wasn't here when Hunter and I dated, or when Hunter left. I'm not sure what I would tell him anyway. That I ran into an old boyfriend and I told him to fuck off, but I'm worried I made a terrible mistake?

I know what Gabe would tell me: he'd tell me I absolutely did the right thing. I'm not sure if that's what I want to hear.

There's a small desk in the guest room, so I've set up a workstation for myself. For the next few days I stay in, working most of the day and watching TV at night. I tell myself I'm not avoiding going out; I'm just busy. But I used to spend at least a few afternoons a week with my laptop at a coffee shop. I don't want to admit it, but I'm afraid of running into Hunter again.

Gabe wasn't kidding when he told me he's not home very much. He leaves each morning before I'm finished with my first cup of coffee. I worry he's become too much of a workaholic since his divorce, but I'm hardly one to be giving life advice.

By Wednesday, I know I need to get out. I'm starting to go stir crazy, shut up inside all day by myself. I reached out to some old friends on social media, but I feel so tentative talking to them. I have no idea what's going on in their lives these days, and I feel guilty for letting our friendships go. And it isn't enough to keep me from the beginnings of some pretty serious cabin fever.

I decide I'll go out for lunch, so I throw on some decent clothes (yes, I've been living in old yoga pants and baggy t-shirts), and try to do something with my hair.

There's a knock at the door, and I stop with the straightener mid-strand. Who could be knocking? As far as I can tell, Gabriel's social life is about as active as mine.

Figuring it's just the UPS guy, I answer the door. It's like walking into a brick wall that I wasn't expecting. I almost bounce backward. Hunter's standing on the doorstep, a couple feet back, as if he knocked and stepped away.

He looks amazing in a dark blue shirt and jeans. Why does he have to be so gorgeous? Why couldn't he have aged badly, instead of morphing into this divine specimen of a man? He was always athletic, but this more mature body is unbelievable.

He smiles at me, as if I didn't treat him like shit the last time I saw him. Not that it was any less than he deserved. Still, I'm so surprised, I gape at him like a moron.

"Hi," he says.

I'm tempted to slam the door in his face, but I have to admit, I don't want to. Curiosity has been eating me alive.

"Hi." I turn so I'm standing with the door partially in front of me. "What are you doing here?"

"I came to ask if you'd like to have coffee with me sometime?"

I swear, he can see right through me. Can he tell how seeing him makes me feel? How torn I am between wanting to slap him and wanting to kiss him?

"I don't know, Hunter," I say.

His expression doesn't change. He looks ... happy. Like he knows a really good secret.

"If you're busy, it doesn't have to be today," he says. "I can't tomorrow, but how about Friday?"

Friday? I look down, my fingers brushing the doorknob. Is there any harm in having coffee with him? Looking at him now, it's harder to feel so angry. Maybe I got it out of my system.

"I guess," I say.

"Great," he says, his tone light. "How about we meet at Old Town Cafe at two on Friday. I'll see you there?"

I find myself nodding. He smiles and walks back to his truck. I can't be sure, but is he limping a little?

"Thanks Emma," he says. "It's good to see you."

"You too."

He smiles again—that ridiculous smile that ruined me when I was sixteen—and drives away.

WHY DID I wait until Friday?

Thursday is literally the longest day ever. I barely get any work done. I should have agreed to have coffee with him when he was here. Then I wouldn't have to spend two days jittery with anticipation. I need to quit being so indecisive.

Of course, I was decisive as hell when he approached me in the parking lot. But I'm not sure that went any better.

I spend half of Friday obsessing over what to wear. I don't want to dress up. I do not want to give him the impression this is a date. It is *not* a date. Two old friends catching up over coffee? Sure. Date? Hell, no. But I don't want to look like crap, either. I'd like to show him what he's been missing all these years.

In the end, I opt for a pair of cropped skinny jeans and a casual green top. I spend a little extra time on my hair, and put on some makeup—just enough that I feel pretty. I want to walk into that coffee shop and make him stare. I want him to remember what I feel like, and see the woman I've become.

I try to hold onto that confidence when I get to Old Town Cafe, but it turns to anxiousness when I see his truck parked out front. I walk inside, the familiar smell of coffee and fresh baked muffins washing over me. Hunter's sitting at a table by the window, and he stands, smiling at me.

I take a quick breath and go to his table.

"Thanks for coming," he says. He still has that look, like he knows something I don't.

"Sure." I take the seat across from him and he sits down.

There are already two cups of coffee on the table, along with a little white pitcher of cream and a container with packets of sweeteners.

"I wasn't sure what you like, so I got you regular coffee," he says. "You can order something else if you want."

"You didn't have to buy my coffee," I say.

He shrugs. "You can get mine next time."

I narrow my eyes at him. Next time? I see what he's doing, but I let it go for now. "So," I say, adding a little cream and half a packet of sugar, "you wanted to meet me."

"I did," he says. "It's been a long time. I thought we could catch up a little."

How can he sound so casual? "Okay, you go first."

He raises his eyebrows, like I caught him off guard, but the look passes almost as quickly as it came. "That's fair. Let's see. I was in the Marines for nine years. I was medically discharged a little over a year ago and came home. Now I work as a private consultant for certain groups in the military, as well as private security firms."

"Okay," I say. "I got a degree in English and now I'm a copy editor for a company that specializes in corporate websites."

"Do you like your job?" he asks.

"Yes, for the most part," I say.

"Did you move back to town recently?" he asks.

He wants me to tell him about my divorce. He must know. "Yes, I did. I recently got divorced."

"I admit, I did hear that," he says. "I hope you're all right."

There's sincerity in his voice that puts a little crack in my distrust. "Thanks. I'm really fine. It was the right thing to do."

He nods. "That's good, then. It's funny that we're both back in town. I didn't think I'd ever live here again, but it's actually nice to be back."

"I won't stay any longer than I have to," I say. Maybe I said that with a little too much enthusiasm.

His eyebrows raise. "That's too bad. It's a nice town."

Are we really going to sit here and talk about the town? "What is the point of this, Hunter?"

"Honestly, Emma, I just want to catch up," he says. "I haven't seen you in a long time. I want to know what's been going on in your life."

I let out a breath. Fine. He wants to know? I'll tell him. "I married a jackass when I was twenty-one and still in college. I knew it was a mistake, but I let my mom pressure me into going through with it, since the wedding was all planned. He didn't want me to work, so I lost years when I could have been building my career. I lost all my friends because he didn't like them. I was miserable, and finally, a little over a year ago, I decided I'd had enough. I left him. He fought me every step of the way, but my divorce was finalized recently. Now I'm broke, but at least I have a good job. The apartment building I was living in should probably be condemned, and I had to move out. I'm moving in with Gabriel because I have nowhere else to go. And then I ran into you."

His casual grin is gone and he stares at me with the pain in his eyes that I saw in the parking lot at Charlie's.

I probably shouldn't have said all that.

"I'm sorry to hear that," he says, his voice soft and quiet. He sounds so genuine, as if he feels like it's his fault.

It is, in a lot of ways. Granted, I made my own choices, but none of it would have happened if he hadn't left.

"So, the Marines," I say, wanting very badly to change the subject. "What was that like?"

"Good for me. Hard. I did some things I'm very proud of, and other things I'm not."

"Why were you discharged?"

"I was in an accident. I broke my pelvis and tore up my knee. Even after three surgeries, I wasn't going to be able to do my job, so that was it."

Holy shit. He *was* limping.

"Wow. What was your job?" I ask.

He opens his mouth and closes it again. "I was a Major. I have to be completely honest, I can't talk about most of it."

"Because it's difficult?" I ask.

"No, because I'm not allowed."

That's ... disturbing. "So what made you come back here?"

He meets my eyes. "It's home."

"I guess that's as good a reason as any."

He starts to reply but his phone rings. "I'm sorry, do you mind if I check that?"

"No, go ahead."

"Thanks." He pulls out his phone. "I need to take this. Excuse me for just a second?"

"Sure."

He stands and walks outside as he answers his phone. I take a sip of coffee. This is so surreal. At some point I should get over my surprise that Hunter is here, but it's hard to get past ten years of not seeing him—ten years of wondering where he was, or if he was ever coming back.

He's only gone for a minute or two. "Sorry about that," he says as he sits down.

"It's fine." I'm curious who it was, but it's definitely none of my business.

We chat for a while longer. He asks questions about my job and my family. I tell him how my dad left my mom when I was twenty, and married some woman he met on a business trip. How I got my job and hid it from Wyatt for a year. He seems impressed by that one. I talk about the disasters in my crappy apartment.

He shares a few things, but I can tell he's choosing his words carefully when he tells me about his time in the Marines. He talks about basic training, and some of the places he's been. He compares the food to torture, and tells me stories of the awful places he's had to sleep. He talks about his family here: his brothers, and his parents. I realize I miss his family. They were really sweet.

I pick up my mug, but it's empty. Again. We've been through three refills as we chat. Hunter sits back and checks the time on his phone.

"I should probably let you get back to your afternoon," he says.

I hesitate. I almost don't want to admit it, but it feels good to talk to him. I kept asking questions just to keep the conversation going. I don't want to stop listening to his voice.

"Yeah, I should probably get some more work done before I call it a day."

"Would you be willing to give me your number?" he asks. "That way I won't have to get my future sister-in-law to help me stalk you if I want to hang out again."

I can't help but laugh. "Yeah, that was a little strange." I pause for a moment. Do I want to give him my number? It isn't like he doesn't know how to find me at this point, but giving him my phone number seems like a step forward. As nice as this was, I'm not interested in stepping anywhere ... with anyone.

But it's just my number. I give it to him and he types it into his phone.

"Tell you what," he says, "I'll text you so you have mine, just in case."

My phone lights up with his text. Why does that make my stomach do a belly flop?

"Thanks."

He smiles at me again and stands up. He lets me go first, and I head out the door, stopping in front of my car.

"Thanks for meeting me," he says. "It was good to see you, Emma."

"Yeah, you too."

My heart starts to beat faster. Is he going to shake my hand? Hug me? Kiss my cheek? I'm torn. I want him to touch me so badly that I almost step forward and hug him. But I'm also terrified to make any sort of physical contact.

But he doesn't approach; he just smiles and walks to his truck. "See you around."

Then he gets in, leaving me standing in front of my car, and drives away.

## 9

## HUNTER

*W*alking away from Emma is so hard. She looks a little bewildered as I say goodbye in front of her car, and I want to hug her so bad. I want to gather her up in my arms and feel her warm body. I want to find her mouth with mine and kiss her like she's never been kissed—even by me.

I want to do a lot of things, but I don't do any of them. I have to be patient with her. Despite the way she stood, lifting her chin just slightly as if she'd accept my lips against hers, I know it's way too soon. Throughout our whole conversation, she fluctuated between closed off and comfortable, holding back and relaxing. One minute, she'd share something fairly personal—like how her dad left her mom. The next, she'd pull back again, clearly unsure of how much she should tell me.

Honestly, I felt the same way. There are some things I can't tell her no matter what, and other things I simply won't. I have memories I don't want to revisit. But it was so easy to open up to her. Despite the way my cock kept trying to distract me, it was easy to stay relaxed.

The strange thing is, it wasn't like old times. We've both changed. I know I'm not the same angry eighteen-year-old, and she's different, too. I suppose we're both older and a little wiser, but she's also a lot more cynical.

It's hard to blame her. I certainly didn't do anything for her confidence in relationships, and she's just getting out of a failed marriage.

It's tempting to text her right away, but I hold back. She doesn't text me either, although I don't expect her to. I can tell she isn't going to make a move. For now, it's me driving this train. Granted, if she surprises me and asks to get together, I certainly won't refuse. But I'm pretty sure it will have to be me who makes contact again.

I figure our coffee date was a solid phase two success. She agreed to come, we had a nice time, and went our separate ways. I was glad I beat her there and had a chance to buy her coffee. It was a small thing, but important to me. It made it more of a date. After our talk today, I know she's averse to dating anyone right now. That's another hurdle I'll have to get over.

Still, it's time to move to phase three.

I wait until late Sunday and send her a text. I figure she's more likely to accept if I suggest something on a weekday afternoon, rather than a weekend or an evening. But I decide to take a chance on something more than coffee.

*Hey, Emma. Any chance you want to grab some lunch tomorrow?*

I wait a few minutes, wondering how she'll reply. I start to doubt my choice. I probably should have suggested coffee again.

My phone vibrates. *Sure, I can do lunch. Where and when?*

I smile. Maybe phase three won't take as long as I thought.

*How about Captain's Chowder House at noon?* It's a restaurant with good food, if a little greasy, and it's definitely not fancy. Hardly even date-worthy at all.

*Okay, see you then.*

I MAKE sure to arrive early so I can get a booth in the corner. I'd rather not be distracted by people behind me. I decide not to order for Emma. I'm happy to buy her lunch, but I'll let her pay for her own if she wants. I don't want to come on too strong.

She walks in, and I get to look at her for a brief moment before she sees me. Her hair is pulled up like it was at the market, and she's wearing a blue shirt and long, striped skirt. I adjust my pants before she looks my direction. The sight of her gets my heart rate going and my dick is extremely interested in what's happening. I take a deep breath, smiling when her face turns in my direction.

Fuck, she's beautiful.

She looks tentative, clutching a small handbag in both hands, but she comes over and sits down.

"Hey," I say. "It's good to see you."

"Thanks," she says, "but I don't know if this is such a good idea."

The tone of her voice sets me on edge even more than her words. I try to act casual. "Why not?"

She looks away. "I'm not ready for this. For dating, or anything like that."

"That's fine," I say, keeping my tone light.

"It is?"

"Sure," I say. "This is definitely not a date."

Emma's brow furrows. "Then what is it?"

"Lunch, I guess," I say. "If I was a date, I would have picked you up at your place, for dinner rather than lunch, and I wouldn't have brought you here. Come on, give me a little credit, Ems."

I realize after I speak that I used her nickname, but it doesn't seem to bother her.

Her shoulders relax, and she no longer looks like she's about to run away. "Okay."

We get up and order at the counter. I decide not to offer to pay. If she doesn't want a date, I won't act like we're on one. We go back to our seats and wait for our food.

"So," she says, "since you aren't dating me, does that mean you're dating someone else?"

I love that she asked me that so quickly. "Nope, definitely not dating anyone."

"And you haven't been married?" she asks.

I fight the urge to smile. I want her to be curious about these things. It means she's at least a little bit interested. "Nope."

"I guess I'm the only idiot who got caught up in that mess."

"I don't think you're an idiot," I say. "You married the wrong guy, but look at you now."

She rolls her eyes and shakes her head. "Yeah, look at me. Divorced before I'm thirty."

"Could be worse," I say, meeting her eyes. "You could still be married."

"I suppose," she says. "But I am not making that mistake again."

I know exactly what she means, and I do not like hearing it, but I pretend to be a little dense. "Well, I'm sure you won't marry the wrong guy a second time."

"No, I'm not getting married again," she says. "Not to

anyone. Been there, done that, got the t-shirt. Or the lawyer bills, at least."

I wonder if she's serious, or saying that to gauge my reaction. I decide to keep playing it cool, despite the sudden tightness in my chest. "Sure, I can see that."

"What about you?" she asks. "Did you ever get close with someone?"

"No," I say. "I was overseas too often to maintain a relationship."

She pauses. "It is so weird to be talking to you about this."

"It is a little, isn't it?"

Her hand is on the table and I have to stop myself from reaching out and touching her.

Our food arrives, and the tension eases as we eat. The food isn't bad. I don't usually eat stuff like this—a little salty, a lot greasy—but it tastes pretty good. We chat a bit, and I avoid asking anything too serious.

Just keeping it light. A couple of friends grabbing a bite to eat. Nothing more.

I want more. A lot more. But I keep myself in check.

I eat about half my fries, and drop one back in the basket. "These remind me of that time we drove up to Seattle and ate down by the waterfront."

Emma laughs. "The time the seagull pooped on your sweatshirt?"

"That's exactly the time," I say. "Fucking seagulls."

"Rats with wings," she says.

I'm a little worried about bringing up the past, but she seems okay. "Or that time we went hiking and couldn't find our way back to the parking lot?"

She laughs again. "Oh my god, that was so stressful. We

kept following those stupid seagulls because we were sure they'd head toward water. We were lost for hours."

"I tried pretty hard to pretend I wasn't nervous," I say.

"You were worried?" she asks.

"Hell yeah, I was worried," I say. "I thought for sure we'd end up spending the night out there."

"You seemed so calm," she says.

"Well, you weren't calm, so one of us had to fake it," I say, giving her a wink.

"That was some impressive acting then," she says. "You had me fooled."

"That summer was a lot of fun," I say. "The summer before senior year."

"Yeah, it was," she says.

A little smile graces her lips. I want to kiss her so bad I can almost taste her.

A change crosses her face, and I know why. I'd bet a million dollars she's thinking about the following summer. The first summer I was gone. I need to change the subject. Fast.

"So have you been to the new movie theater in town?" I ask.

"No, I haven't," she says.

"Can you believe they finally built one out here? All those years we had to drive half an hour to see a movie. Kids these days don't know how good they have it."

"They never do," she says.

I sure didn't.

We finish up our meal and I try to judge what my next move should be. She doesn't want a date. I'm not quite sure how to get past that particular declaration. I can ask her out again, but I get the feeling I'll have to keep it in the friend realm if I'm going to get her to agree.

Which is fine. Spending time with her is the goal. I figure I can play along with the non-date-dates thing for a while. She needs a chance to get to know me again. Time is the only way to make that happen.

I grab our mostly empty baskets and clear the table, dumping everything in the trash. Emma heads for the door. Damn it, I don't want this to end, but I can't think of a good excuse to keep her with me today. I need to work up to driving somewhere with her. I hold the door as we leave the restaurant and walk her to her car.

"That was fun, yeah?" I ask.

She stands next to her car door, but I notice she's not getting her keys. "Yeah, it was fun."

So far so good. "I was thinking." I pause and step closer before I quite realize what I'm doing. "Since you haven't been to the new movie theater—"

"No, Hunter." She backs up a step.

*Shit.* "Hey, it's fine," I say. "I get it. No dating. But friends can go to a movie, right?"

"A movie sounds a lot like a date."

"I'm just trying to avoid going to the movies alone and looking like a loser," I say.

She still looks skeptical.

"What if it's a matinee on Saturday, we arrive separately, and pay our own way?" I ask.

She presses her lips together, and a sweet little groove forms between her eyebrows. God, she's adorable, even when she's stressed.

"I'll even let you pick the movie," I say.

She lets out a breath and looks away. "I guess that would be okay."

"Awesome. Well, I suppose you need to get back to work."

I don't think I can resist her closeness anymore. For half a second I consider holding out my hand, but instead I move in for a hug. I don't try to sneak into her personal space. I raise my arms and lift my eyebrows, looking her right in the eyes.

*Can I? Will you let me touch you?*

She makes a cute little noise in her throat, and one side of her mouth turns up. I move closer; she raises her arms. I expect her to go for the over-under hug—each of us with one arm high, the other low—but she puts both arms around my neck and lets me put mine around her waist.

I strain to hold myself in check as she very slowly presses against me. Oh holy fuck, she feels so good. Her scent is light and floral, making my head swim. Her body is firm, and I risk slipping my hands from her narrow waist up to her back. I close my eyes, knowing I have only seconds. I squash every instinct that demands I hold her tighter, turn my face into her hair, press my lips against her neck.

I feel her sharp intake of breath and she pulls away. I drop my arms immediately, despite how my body screams for more. I swallow hard, trying to get my bearings. God, that was so good. I'm itching to grab her and hold her again. I struggle to train my face to stillness and pretend that didn't just rock my world.

"It's good to see you, Emma," I manage to say, although my voice is a bit strained.

"Yeah," she says. It's almost a whisper. Her eyes move across my face, her brow furrowing again.

*Damn it. I shouldn't have touched her yet.*

I give her an easy smile and step back, trying to stay calm, but my heart feels like it's going to beat right out of my chest. *Patience, Hunter. Be patient.*

"I'll see you Saturday," I say. I think I sound pretty

normal, although I desperately hope she does not look down. I can't adjust myself while she's watching, and I'm hard as a fucking rock.

"Right, Saturday," she says. She reaches for her keys, but hesitates.

*Damn it, Emma, you better get in your car right this second.* My self-control is strained so far I'm about to snap. Every bit of me wants to grab her and kiss her until she melts. Fuck phase three. Her body reacted just like mine. I felt it. I could convince her to come home with me, right now. Show her how crazy she's making me. Plunge my hard cock into her and remind her how good we were together. How good we could be again.

She opens her car door, and reality smacks me upside the head. I hold up my hand as she backs out of her parking spot, as if I didn't just imagine fucking the shit out of her in my bed.

I let out a heavy breath and get in my truck. I'm definitely going to have to jack off when I get home. My cock is pissed off at this point.

Patience is going to be harder than I thought.

## 10

## EMMA

*D*amn you, Hunter.

I am *not* falling for you again. I'm not falling for anyone. I am done with dating. Done with men. End of story.

But as I drive away from him, I'm practically clenching my thighs. His arms around me felt like the best thing in the entire world. All the wine and coffee and chocolate and cozy blankets ever made, all rolled into one set of muscular arms and a strong chest. His hands touched my waist, slid around my back. He was so familiar. So safe.

No. He is *not* safe. Not by a long shot.

I shouldn't have agreed to go to a movie with him. What was I thinking? I wasn't, that's the problem. That's not true. I was. I was thinking about those eyes, that body, those hands all over me. About that mouth and what it would feel like on my skin. About the hardness of his cock, which I could totally see through his pants.

I blow out a long breath and try to ignore the throbbing between my legs. It's so unfair that he can do that to me. He

backed off like he wasn't even fazed by that hug. He just
waved goodbye, like we're nothing more than friends.

But isn't that what I want?

*This is ridiculous.*

I go home and force myself to focus on work. Gabriel
and I are taking tomorrow to move my stuff out of my apartment, so I need to get ahead on my latest editing project. I
work until well after ten, then call it a night when Gabe gets
home.

Lying in bed, I can't think of anything but Hunter. He
still smelled the same. Sort of rugged, but clean. I don't
think he wears cologne, it's just the scent of his body mixed
with the Right Guard deodorant he still wears. I used to
borrow his t-shirts just to keep that smell nearby. I never
told him, but I slept with one on my pillow most of the time
we were dating.

There's a little bit of that scent lingering on my shirt. I
don't bother changing out of it. I fall asleep with thoughts of
Hunter flooding my mind, his scent in my nose.

The next morning, Gabe and I get an early start. He
rents a moving truck and we drive out to Cedar Falls, about
forty minutes from Jetty Beach. I don't have a lot of stuff—
I'm still rebuilding after leaving Wyatt—but I do have a few
pieces of furniture. We pull up to the apartment building
and I drop off the letter giving my official move-out notice.
Then we head around to the back of the complex. We're
lucky enough to find a decent parking spot, and I haul some
moving boxes upstairs.

There's a letter taped to the door. Great, I wonder what
they found this time. Spiders? Rats? Does the building need
new siding, or did the roof cave in? I grab the letter and
bring it inside, but I toss it on the top of the mail basket. I'm

leaving, so I don't need to worry about whatever apartment drama is happening this time.

We pack what we can, and start hauling things to the truck. Around noon, I grab us some lunch; after we eat, we get back to work. I almost forgot how much moving sucks. I might not have a lot of stuff, but it takes us most of the day to get everything out. I don't worry about cleaning too much. I figure my deposit is a sunk cost at this point, and decide to let it go.

I run back upstairs to make sure we didn't miss anything. I grab my purse and the letter that was taped to the door. I'm about to leave it on the counter, when I decide to see what it says.

*Emma,*

*I think we still have some unfinished business. I'm not sure how things went so wrong, but I'm sorry. I'd really like to see you. Give me a call.*

*Wyatt*

A sick feeling uncurls in the pit of my stomach. I crumple the paper and toss it in the sink. There is no way I'm calling him.

I get out to the truck and slam the door closed.

"You okay?" Gabe asks.

"Not really," I say. "There was a note from Wyatt on the door."

Gabe clenches the steering wheel. "I thought he didn't know where you live."

"I guess he found out. I haven't seen him in a few months, so I wasn't sure."

"Well, look on the bright side," Gabe says. "You're out now. He can tape notes to that door all he wants."

I laugh. Gabe has a good point. "I hope some big, dangerous biker dude moves in and Wyatt knocks on the door."

"That would be awesome." He glances at me again. "Are you sure you're okay?"

"Yeah," I say. "I won't let him get to me anymore."

"Good."

Hunter, on the other hand, that's another story.

We get my stuff to Gabe's place and unload most of it into the garage. It's late by the time we're finished, and we both go to bed, exhausted.

I don't even hear Gabe leave the next day. I spend the morning working, but by mid-afternoon I know I'm done for. My ability to concentrate is completely gone. The note from Wyatt shook me up more than I want to admit. I wonder how long it will take before he realizes I don't live there. Maybe he even drove by and saw the moving truck. I wouldn't put it past him, especially considering he went to the trouble to try to contact me.

I need a drink. I feel a little guilty for the dent I've put in Gabe's wine stash, but I make sure to choose something that doesn't look expensive. I'll find a way to make it up to him later. I pour a glass and go out to the back porch.

Fucking Wyatt.

And then it hits me.

I don't really care that Wyatt left a note, or that he figured out where I was living. I'm obsessing over that stupid letter to keep my mind off what's really bothering me: Hunter.

Why do I let these men have this kind of power over me?

I've been so desperate to keep Hunter off my mind, I've resorted to thinking about Wyatt. How pathetic am I?

All the changes in my life come crashing down on me. My divorce. Leaving my apartment. Seeing Hunter. It's all so much. I cover my face with my hands and let out a groan.

It's been a while since I've gotten properly drunk, and I decide now is the time. Gabe has a well-stocked liquor cabinet, so I pull out a bottle of tequila. If I'm going to do this, I might as well do it right.

Several shots later (I've honestly lost track), I stumble over to the couch and try to get the TV to turn on. I can't seem to find the *on* button, which is inexplicably hilarious. It's slightly less funny when I realize I'm drunk off my ass and very alone. And it's four in the afternoon.

I lean my head back against the cushions and close my eyes. The burning liquid gold didn't do anything to take my mind off Hunter. Those hands. That mouth. I've never forgotten the way his body felt. We were practically kids the last time we were together, and it's been so long, but I start getting wet just thinking about him. God, his arms felt good the other day. I was so tempted to kiss him. Right now, I can't quite remember why I didn't.

What am I so afraid of? We're two adults. We aren't a couple of stupid teenagers anymore. When he had his arms around me, all I could think about was how much I wanted more.

Maybe that *no men* thing was a little harsh. No men? Ever? No dating, no relationships—fine. But a woman has needs. And right now, my needs are burning me up inside.

He gave me his number. So why the fuck not? I'd bet money he wants me too. I'll just make it clear that this isn't an invitation to date me. I just want to get laid. And hell, we've even done it before. If we get it out of the way, maybe when we hang out at the movies this weekend there won't be so much tension. This is the perfect solution.

I fumble with my phone and send him a text. *You should really come over.*

I giggle at my own genius. Why didn't I think of this sooner?

He texts back. *U OK?*

I smile and cover my mouth to stifle a hiccup. *I will be once you get here.*

*I thought we have plans Saturday?*

Come on, Hunter. Don't make me spell it out. Hiccup. *I don't want to wait. You should come. Now.*

Less than ten minutes later, I hear his truck outside.

## 11

## HUNTER

My gut tells me I'm going way outside protocol. But fuck, man, I'm pretty sure I know what her texts mean. Am I really supposed to resist?

I sit outside her house for a minute. Why the sudden change of heart? We had lunch two days ago. Has she been thinking about that hug all this time? I've had a hard time thinking of anything else, so it's possible. But why now?

I go up to her door, feeling like I'm walking into a trap. But I'm here. I might as well see where this goes. I knock, and Emma opens the door, dressed in nothing but a long t-shirt. It brushes the tops of her thighs, barely hiding her panties.

Oh, fucking hell.

"Hey," she says, leaning against the door. It swings open a little more and she stumbles to the side.

Son of a bitch. She's drunk.

I let out a sigh and my shoulders slump. That's why. It's not a change of heart. She doesn't want to let me in. She wants something, all right, judging by the way she's looking at me. Her eyes are half closed and she bites her lip.

Fuck, this sucks. It sucks big fat donkey balls, and I have no idea if I can make it out of here in one piece. I need to turn around right this second and leave. She'll thank me once she sleeps this off.

She grabs my wrist.

*Shit.*

"Come inside," she says, tugging on my arm.

Her hand is warm against my skin. I don't want to pull away, but I do, disengaging from her grasp.

"I don't think this is a good idea, Ems," I say.

"Yes, it definitely is," she says. "You should come in. I want you to."

"You think you want me to, but I don't know if you'll feel the same way tomorrow."

My dick and my brain engage in an epic battle of wills. I could have her, right now. I could push her inside and rip off that shirt. She'd let me. I could fuck her until she begs for mercy.

There's even a part of me that tries to argue that this might work. This might move things along. We'll have such amazing sex, she'll sober up and still want me. I'll sleep next to her and she'll wake me up with a hand job, wanting more. I'll fuck her right into phase four.

She hiccups and covers her face with her hand. She's so unsteady, she's practically swaying on her feet. She has no idea what she's doing right now.

I don't want her like this.

"Okay, Ems, you need to go lie down," I say.

Her bottom lip quivers and tears flood her eyes. "You don't want me?"

I clench my teeth. I'm supposed to be keeping things in the friend zone. If I don't tread very carefully, I'm going to ruin the progress I've already made. I'll probably find myself at phase negative five.

"Come on," I say. I step inside and put an arm around her shoulders. She stumbles as I walk her to the couch. "There you go, lie down."

She does what I ask, and I cover her up with a blanket. Tears spill down her cheeks. "What are you doing?"

"I'm getting you some water."

I grab the bottle of tequila and the shot glass off the coffee table and put them in the kitchen. Then I get her a glass of water. She sits up and I hand her the glass, making sure she doesn't spill.

I sit on the floor next to her. "How much tequila did you drink?"

She shrugs. "Don't know. A lot."

"I can tell."

She sniffs and takes another sip of water. "I loved it when you hugged me the other day."

Oh, man. I wonder if she's going to remember this tomorrow. I can't tell. "Yeah, me too."

"You did?" she asks.

"Of course I did."

"It didn't seem like it," she says.

I look away. "Ems, you've had a lot of tequila."

"So?" *Hiccup.* "I'm still me."

"Yes, you are," I say. "But you're not acting like yourself."

She sits forward, leaning close. I can smell the tequila on her, but far from being unpleasant, it makes me want to run my tongue along her lips and lick the last of it off.

"You should kiss me, Hunter," she says.

Why is she making this so hard? "You don't really want me to."

"I do," she says. "I really do."

"No." I put a hand on her shoulder and gently nudge her back. "The tequila wants me to kiss you. You made it very clear you don't want to date anyone."

"Who said anything about dating?" She flops back and leans her head against the cushion. "I didn't ask you over here to take me out to dinner."

"Ems, if we do this now, you're only going to regret it later," I say.

"There's nothing to regret," she says. Her voice is clear. I can almost convince myself she's sobering up. "We're adults. We're both single. It's not even something we haven't done before." She pulls the blanket to the side, exposing one of her bare legs. "Aren't you curious? Do you remember what I feel like?"

Oh fuck. Fuck, fuck, fuck. "Ems..."

She moves the blanket across her lap and tilts her knees open.

I want to. I want to run my hands up those thighs, bury my face between her legs. Fuck, I want to.

But I can't.

I push her legs back together and pull the blanket across her lap. Her brow furrows, and her lower lip trembles again.

"Don't cry," I say.

She breaks out into a choking sob. "Why did you leave me?"

Oh god. "We can't do this right now."

"Why? I have to know. Was I so awful that you had to get away from me?"

I know I shouldn't touch her again, but I slip my hand over hers and squeeze. "No, Emma. It wasn't you. I swear."

"Then why?"

"Let's talk after you sober up," I say, my voice firm. I'm still holding her hand. I can't let go.

She looks into my eyes and tears run down her cheeks, spilling from the corners. I want to die right here. Suddenly my plan seems ridiculous. How can we possibly get past all the pain I caused her? I was such an idiot to think she could forgive me. She won't spend the rest of her life looking at the man who did that to her, who gave her that haunted look in her eyes.

I'd love to believe it wasn't me, that it was her ex-husband. But I know I'm kidding myself. It *was* me. I did this to her.

I let go of her hand and give her the glass of water. "Finish this and get more when you're ready to get up," I say. "I'm sorry, Ems, I have to go."

I can't look at her again.

Mission aborted.

## 12

### EMMA

*M*y stomach roils, and I try to bury myself deeper into the mattress—only it doesn't feel like I'm in bed. I crack open one eye, just as a test. Pain stabs through my head.

This is definitely not good.

I roll over and my leg sticks out over nothing. I'm not in bed. Where the fuck am I? My eyes fly open in a moment of panic. What did I do? I didn't leave the house, did I?

No, I'm on Gabe's couch. I must have fallen asleep here —or passed out, technically.

I suddenly remember why it's been so long since I got that drunk.

I sit up and put a hand to my forehead. Tequila is not my friend. Why did I do that to myself? I get up and grab the water glass sitting on the coffee table. I need more of that. And then maybe I'll consider food. Possibly.

I push the glass against the water dispenser in the freezer door and my eyes widen. I didn't get myself water last night. I don't think Gabe did either. He worked so late, I don't even remember him coming home.

It was Hunter.

*Oh no.*

Hazy memories come back to me. I texted him, didn't I? I realize I'm only half dressed. Oh shit, did we? I search my memory. I don't feel like I had sex recently. In fact, the way I feel even thinking about having sex makes me pretty sure it's been a long time.

But he was here, wasn't he?

I check my phone and see that I did indeed invite him over. I sit down on the couch and take a drink of water. Yep, now I remember. I texted that very obvious invitation, and he showed up.

I remember thinking it all sounded so logical. Why not have a little no strings sex with my ex-boyfriend? What could that hurt?

Fuck, tequila makes me stupid.

And then I threw myself at him, and he rejected me.

I don't know how to feel about that.

On the one hand, thank God he did.

On the other hand, I was half-naked and very willing, and he left. Why did he leave? Was he trying to be a gentleman? Or has he been serious this whole time about only wanting to hang out as friends?

Wow, I managed to make a mess of this, didn't I?

My head is killing me, so I get up and take some ibuprofen. I know I should call Hunter and apologize, but I avoid it by taking a shower and getting some breakfast.

My delay has the advantage of giving my headache time to ease and I no longer feel in danger of puking. Texting him is probably a cop-out, but I'm so tempted. I could send him a quick message. *Sorry about last night. Tequila, right?*

Instead, I bring up his number, close my eyes, and call.

But he doesn't answer.

Shit.

His voicemail picks up. What should I say? I can't apologize in a message. But hanging up without saying anything is probably just as bad. His message ends, and I hear the beep.

"Hi, it's Emma. Can you, um ... can you call me back? Thanks."

I hang up, wondering if he will. Are we still on for Saturday? I don't even know.

A few days ago, I would have told myself this was a good thing. It doesn't matter who he is, or what kind of history we have—I do *not* need a man in my life. Even if it's Hunter. Especially if it's Hunter.

Now, I'm not so sure.

～

HUNTER DOESN'T CALL me back. Saturday morning dawns and I haven't heard a word from him. I've thought about texting or calling him again. What if he didn't get my message? What if he got busy and forgot? But I know that's not the case. He doesn't want to talk to me.

I'm a mixture of angry and embarrassed. Angry that he's ignoring me when all I want to do is apologize, embarrassed that it's necessary in the first place.

At eleven, I decide to text him. We were supposed to meet at the movie theater at noon. I assume that's off, but I also don't want to be the one who doesn't show up. Or the one who gets stood up.

*Hey. Haven't heard from you. Are we still on for today?*

The wait for his reply seems like hours. Just tell me,

damn it. All this anticipation, this not knowing, is driving me up the wall. Be straight with me, Hunter.

*Sure, if you want.*

If I want? What does that mean? I hate feeling like we're playing some stupid game. This is why I said no dating. I don't need this bullshit in my life.

But I still show up at the theater at noon.

I'm wearing layered green and white tank tops and a chevron print skirt. I stand outside the ticket window, looking for him. At first I don't think he's coming. It's twelve, like we said, and the last couple times I met him somewhere, he arrived first. My heart sinks. I don't want to admit how much I want to see him, but my disappointment level is pretty high. I get my phone out of my purse to see if he texted.

"Hey, sorry I'm late."

I gasp at his voice and look up. He looks utterly perfect in a gray shirt and jeans.

"That's okay," I say. "For a second, I wondered if you were coming."

He shrugs. "I invited you. What are we seeing?"

Crap, I haven't even thought about that. I glance at the choices. It's a small theater, so there aren't many options. I choose one that's starting soon.

"Sounds good," he says. He goes to the ticket booth and buys himself a ticket.

I don't care about paying, but I can't help but feel a flash of disappointment that he didn't offer. Of course, why would he? Drunken antics aside, I've made it very clear that I don't want a date. He's simply respecting my wishes. I should be happy about that.

I buy my ticket and follow him in. I wish he would stop for half a second so I can apologize for the other night, but he goes right to the concession counter. I come up next to him and nudge him with my elbow.

"Can I buy the snacks?"

He shrugs. "If you want. I just want a water."

"No popcorn?" I ask.

He glances at me, his eyes searching. Like he's trying to figure me out.

I smile. "I'll get a bucket and you can have some if you want."

He nods, and I order the popcorn and two bottled waters, then follow him into the theater. We get seats in the middle, right where we always used to sit. For the first time, thinking about the past doesn't make me feel ill. It's a sweet memory, and I can recall it untainted by the way our relationship ended.

We settle in, and I take a few bites of popcorn. When the previews begin I start to get worried; these movies all look awful. After the last preview—a groan-worthy family drama that looks like a great way to get in a nap—I look over at Hunter, raising my eyebrows. Back when we were younger, we used to critique all the previews.

I lean closer. "That looked awful. I hope I didn't pick a horrible movie."

"It was pretty bad," he says.

The movie is worse than I feared. It's boring and slow. About halfway through, I realize I'm eating the entire tub of popcorn by myself. I tip it in his direction and he takes a handful.

"Are you as bored as I am?" I ask.

"I was wondering if it was just me," he says.

Boring or not, I'm having a hard time focusing on the movie. I think about how Hunter has treated me since I first saw him in the parking lot at Charlie's. He's been sweet and kind, polite. It's like he's being patient with me, giving me what I need to feel at ease with him. It's part of what's so disarming. He's so different. Back in high school, he was darker. Angrier. He never took it out on me; he treated me like spun sugar. But he was intense, and he had a quick temper. This older Hunter is so much calmer. The depth is still there, but he seems more relaxed. More at home in his own skin.

Maybe it's maturity. Or maybe he went through something he needed to experience in order to get here.

I move the popcorn toward him again. "Sorry, I didn't know what this movie was when I picked it." I pause, hesitating. "I guess you get to pick next time."

I watch him from the corner of my eye to see how he reacts to my *next time* comment. His eyes don't leave the screen, but the corner of his mouth turns up in a smile. He grabs a handful of popcorn and tosses it at me.

"You're definitely not allowed to pick movies anymore," he says.

I laugh and lean closer to him. "Hunter, I'm so sorry about the other night."

"Don't be," he says. "It's not a big deal."

"Thanks for taking care of me, even though I was a drunk mess."

He shifts so he's closer to me. "All I did is get you water."

I settle in so our shoulders are touching. I want to lay my head against him, but I can't quite make myself do it. "Well, it was a nice thing to do. I'm so sorry I put you in that position."

He presses his lips together in small smile and shakes his head. "I'm sorry if I hurt your feelings. Leaving you like that was literally one of the hardest things I've ever done in my entire life."

A tingle runs down my spine. Does that mean he did want me?

"I'm sorry I didn't return your call," he says. "You threw me off. I wasn't sure what to do."

"It's okay," I say. "Thanks for still hanging out with me today."

"Yeah. It's good to see you."

He reaches for the popcorn and our hands brush. My body lights up, electricity running through my veins. I'm sixteen again, on our first date, desperately wishing he'd hold my hand. We touch and my heart races.

The back of his hand rests against mine. He doesn't look at me, but slides his hand between my palm and the popcorn bucket. I move the popcorn with my other hand while he entwines his fingers with mine.

I breathe so fast I get a little dizzy. My hand fits in his perfectly. My forearm rests on top of his and he watches the screen, holding my hand.

I have no idea what happens during the rest of the movie. His hand is large and strong, and he doesn't let go. I work up the courage to rest my cheek against his shoulder. I wonder if he might kiss me—my lips tingle with the anticipation of it—but he doesn't turn toward me. The movie ends and he lets go of my hand. I miss his touch instantly, but I gather up my purse and follow him outside.

I want him to hold my hand again as we walk, but he doesn't. I'm jittery, wondering what happens now. Should I make another move? Should I try to kiss him?

I want him so desperately—but, after the other night, I'm afraid to say anything. Granted, I'm sober, which clearly makes a difference. But what if he says no?

He stops on the sidewalk outside the theater. "So, I'm parked over there."

The disappointment is crushing. Is this it? But wait, what else do I want from him? I'm not supposed to want a man again. I've been there, done that. Once with this very man, and it crashed and burned in the worst way. But in this moment, the only thing I want is to stay with him, even just a little longer.

We get all the way to my car before I find the courage to speak. "Are you hungry?"

He looks at me, his eyes curious. "Are you, after all that popcorn?"

I'm actually not, but I'm panicking. I just don't want him to go. "I guess I'm not, really," I say. "Maybe coffee, then?"

He pauses, looking away, like he's thinking. "I would really love to, but I can't. I have somewhere to be this afternoon. I'm already running late."

"Oh, I'm sorry," I say, trying not to let my disappointment show. "I didn't realize."

"No, of course you didn't," he says. "Believe me, I'd cancel if I could. I'd love nothing more than to spend the rest of the day with you."

His eyes don't leave my face and my belly flip flops.

"Maybe, um..." *Say something, Emma. Tell him you'll go on a real date. A date doesn't have to mean you're getting serious.* "Maybe we could have dinner sometime? Something a little more ... like a date?"

One corner of his mouth turns up. "Are you sure?"

"Yeah," I say. "I'm sure."

He picks up my hand, and I shiver. "Tomorrow?"

"That would be great," I manage to say, although I feel like my voice is giving out.

He brings my hand to his lips and kisses my fingers. My knees almost buckle. He holds my hand close to his mouth, and I can feel his breath across my fingers. "It was really good to see you, Emma."

"You too."

He smiles again and walks to his truck, leaving me absolutely breathless.

## 13

## HUNTER

*I* want to stay with Emma. She's melting for me, faster than I thought possible. I can feel her walls breaking down. I know I still need to be careful, so it's probably better that I have to go. But walking away from her after the movie is as hard as it was the other night.

I feel bad for not calling her back after her little tequila stunt, but like I told her, she threw me off. It wasn't that she got smashed and suggested we have sex. That I could deal with. And fuck, it was tempting.

What killed me was the look in her eyes when she asked me why I left her. I'm still not sure what to do with that. Drunk or not, that pain was real, and I'm the one who caused it. Ten years later, she's still hurt. The wounds I left were deep. When it comes down to it, I have no idea if we can recover from that. I hope she can bring herself to forgive me, but after seeing her face the other night, I'm not sure she can.

When she texted me earlier, I was tempted to tell her no. But the movie was my idea, and I already felt like a jackass for ignoring her for the last couple days. Besides, I wanted to see her. I'd like to think I had some gentlemanly motive for meeting her at the movies—give her a chance to clear the air after the other night—but really, it was entirely selfish. I missed her, and I couldn't say no to the chance to be with her again.

I thought about holding her hand for the first half of the movie. Cheesy? Yeah, probably. I certainly had our first date in mind when I asked her to go to a movie. She didn't want a date, so we went to a matinee and I didn't buy her ticket. But as far as I was concerned, it would be a date by the time it was over. Even if all I did was hold her hand. Just like the first time.

And fuck, it felt good. It was like being a nervous kid again. I brushed my hand against hers on purpose and I almost jumped out of my seat. A burst of sensation went straight to my chest, sucking the air from my lungs. I didn't spend the next ten minutes working my way up to actually holding her hand the way I did when we were sixteen. I moved with a little more authority this time, although I still stopped at hand-holding.

My self-control is being severely tested lately.

I take a few breaths to calm down as I drive away. If I hadn't planned to see Isaac today, that date would not be over. But I can't let my little buddy down.

I have a great time with Isaac, and Elaine looks better than last week, so I feel good about my decision.

And Emma agreed to a real date tomorrow. I have that to look forward to.

Sunday, I debate where I should take her, and decide on Stewart's Seafood House. It's a nice place with a great view, but not so fancy as to be stuffy. I dress up a bit, putting on a nice pair of slacks and a dark green sweater. On the way to pick her up, I make a quick stop at Charlie's for flowers. If this is a date, I'm going to do it right.

She answers the door in a black dress with a low neckline. I stare at her for a moment, speechless.

"You look incredible," I say, handing her the flowers.

She smiles. "These are beautiful. Thank you."

I wait in the doorway while she puts the flowers in the kitchen. When she's ready, I walk her to my truck and open the door for her. We drive to the restaurant and I hold her hand on the way inside. I try to keep my face still, but I can't stop smiling. I feel like we're inches from phase four.

Dinner is great, and our conversation is relaxed and easy. Natural. I can't stop staring at her. Her hair is curled in soft waves that frame her face, and her dress shows her collarbone and the tops of her breasts. I don't want to push her too far tonight, but my skin prickles with every breath she takes.

After dessert, I walk her back to the truck. I'm not remotely ready for this night to end, but I'm not sure I should suggest going to my place. Things still feel tenuous, and so far this has been an absolutely perfect date. I don't want to ruin it. I open the door for her, smelling her hair as she gets in. God, she smells good.

I get in and make a snap decision. "Are you up for a drink?"

"Yeah," she says, without hesitation. "It doesn't have to be fancy. We could just go to Danny's."

"Great," I say, hoping my brothers aren't there. Clover texts me every other day, asking what's going on with Emma, but so far I've kept my answers vague. I'm not ready to share this with anyone yet. I don't want to jinx it.

Danny's Tavern is pretty dead, and I'm grateful I don't see anyone I recognize. We find a table and I go to the bar to order us drinks—a glass of Jack Daniels for me and a Cabernet for Emma. When I sit down, I find Emma staring at the bar, her face ashen.

"Ems, what's wrong?" I ask. I glance over. There's a guy sitting at the bar, but I don't know who he is. "Do you know him?"

"That's Wyatt."

Instantly, my blood burns hot. What the fuck is her ex-husband doing here? I stand up, placing myself in between them so he can't see her. "Let's go."

She swallows hard and nods. I take her hand as she gets up and keep myself positioned in Wyatt's line of sight. I wrap a protective arm around her shoulders, not caring for a second whether I'm intruding on her personal space.

We get out the door, and she's shaking.

"You're okay." I draw her in closer to me as we walk. "We'll be out of here in ten seconds."

Behind us, someone speaks. "Emma."

She stops, and I keep my arm tight around her. I turn and look at Wyatt. He's standing in the doorway to the bar, dressed in a dark shirt and jeans. I note his size and the set of his feet. He's smaller than I am, which could mean he's fast, but the way he's standing tells me I'll own him in two seconds flat if it comes down to it. I hope it doesn't, but if he fucks with her, I'll rip his arms off.

"Do you want to go?" I ask quietly.

"Emma, I just want to talk," Wyatt says. "Just for a minute."

The nerve of this guy. I want to remind this jackass that Emma fucking divorced him, but I decide to wait and see what she does.

She takes a deep breath, and when she speaks, her voice

is steady. "No, it's okay. I can talk to him. He isn't dangerous or anything. He's just kind of a dick."

"Are you sure?" I ask.

"Yeah, just to get it over with," she says. "I want to know what the fuck he's doing here and make sure he doesn't come back."

I smile at the moxie in her voice. That's my girl. I step aside and let my arm drop.

"What do you want, Wyatt?" she asks.

"Just five minutes, babe," he says.

I clench my hands into fists. If he calls her *babe* again, I'll break his face.

"We're divorced, Wyatt," she says. "You can call me Emma. Ms. Parker, if you try calling me babe again."

"Fine, *Emma*," he says, emphasizing her name. "Can we talk? Alone?"

She gives me a nod and I wait while she walks toward a red sedan. I cross my arms and stare Wyatt down.

*Please, you fucker. Give me a reason.*

They stand in front of the car, facing each other. Emma keeps her distance, backing up when he takes a step toward her. I can't hear what they're saying, but Emma looks exasperated. She shakes her head. He raises his arms, gesturing. I stand still, my eyes locked on Wyatt. I keep my breathing even. My mind is clear, calm. I'm a spring, coiled up and ready to strike.

She crosses her arms and shakes her head again. He takes a step forward and I almost dart in. But Emma holds up a hand and I see the word *No* on her lips. Wyatt's gaze darts to me. I can see his anger written across his face. She might not think he's dangerous, but I know that look. Desperation. That will make any man dangerous, even a dicksock like Wyatt.

I see it begin as if everything is in slow motion: Emma starts to walk away, and Wyatt grabs her wrist. She tries to pull her arm back and I hear her voice, high-pitched and angry. He doesn't let go.

In four strides, I'm there. I grab his forearm, hard. His hand opens, freeing Emma, and she steps back. I wrench his arm around his back and smash him down onto the hood of his car. I push against his arm, just enough to show I can break it if I want to.

His face contorts with pain. "What the fuck!"

I lean down and speak in a low voice. "If you touch her again, you'll be lucky if all I break is your arm." I increase the pressure to drive the point home, holding him there for a few more seconds. "Now, I'm going to let you up. You're going to get in your car and go. And you are never, ever going to bother her again. Understood?"

I can feel his defiance. This guy is something else. I think of twenty more ways I can hurt him with my bare hands—and if he so much as looks at Emma again, I'm going to do at least ten of them.

"Do I have to break it to prove I'm serious?" I ask, wrenching his arm harder. He cries out in pain. I lean closer and lower my voice so Emma can't hear. "You wouldn't be my first kill, asshole."

He goes limp, and I know I scared the fight out of him. I let go and he stands. I step back, crossing my arms. I'm pleased to see he doesn't look in Emma's direction. She moves behind me and I stay where I am, my feet planted. Wyatt gets in his car and drives away. I watch him go, my eyes on his car until he's out of sight.

Emma has a hand over her mouth. I breathe out the last of my aggression, and pull her into my arms. She doesn't resist. I can feel her shoulders shake.

*Fuck, I probably scared her.*

I hold her close, rubbing her back. Her face is buried in my chest, her hand clutching my shirt.

"Damn it, Ems, I'm sorry," I say. "It pissed me off when he grabbed you."

She shakes her head, but doesn't pull away from me. "It's okay. I'm just overwhelmed."

"Why don't we get out of here. I'll get you home."

I really don't want to take her home, but I feel like it's the right thing to do. She's pretty shaken up.

We get in my truck and I head toward her place. It's hard to keep still. The adrenaline coursing through my system has me on edge. I have to work to keep from breathing hard, and my heart thumps uncomfortably.

"I don't want to go home," she says, her voice quiet. "Can we go to your place?"

A jolt shoots through me and I grip the steering wheel to keep my hands from shaking. My dick gets hard, instantly. The combination of adrenaline and sudden arousal is almost more than I can handle. I don't trust myself to talk, so I nod, and drive to my place in silence.

I park in my driveway and hesitate. Emma's hands are clasped in her lap. I need to say something. I have to make sure this is okay.

"Are you sure you want to come in?" I ask.

"Yes." There's no hesitation in her voice.

She gets out before I can come around to open her door. I put my hand on her back as we head inside, even the casual touch through her clothes lighting me up. I close the door behind us, and like a rope snapping, my self-control is gone.

I turn and pin her against the door. Her purse drops. She lifts her chin and I claim her mouth. It's mine, every bit of it.

I press her against the door with my body, letting my hard cock dig into her. Her hands slide around to the back of my neck and she kisses me, her lips as hungry as mine.

She grabs my shirt, still damp with her tears, and lifts it. I pull it off, letting it fall. She runs her hands along my chest and down my abs to my pants. I wrap my arms around her, pulling her into me, and trail hard kisses down her neck.

My uninhibited need for her takes over. I find the hem of her dress and hike it up, grabbing her ass. I kiss her again, deep. Her tongue is firm against mine. I'm bursting with too much adrenaline, and I'm in danger of losing control. I grab her panties at the waistband with both hands and pull apart. The fabric rips and I let them drop. Her hands fumble with the button of my pants. She gets them undone and I slide them down, kicking them off to the side.

She plunges her hand into my underwear and wraps her fingers around my cock. A haze tinges my vision and I push one of her arms above her head, pinning it to the door. Her other hand holds my dick in a vice like grip. My mouth meets hers, our tongues lashing against each other, hard and aggressive.

I slip my other hand between her thighs and feel her wetness. The feel of her on my fingers makes me crazy with desire.

"I need to be inside you," I say, my voice a growl. "Right fucking now."

I grab her ass and lift her up, pushing her against the door. She wraps her legs around me and I plunge my cock inside her.

Holy fuck. I'm undone. She's slick and hot, and the moan she lets out almost makes me come right there. She leans her head back, her eyes closed. I thrust my hips, sliding in and out of her wet pussy, and bury my face in her neck. God, she feels so good. I've never felt anyone like her. She clings to my back, digging her fingers into my skin, and calls out. Her voice is raw and uninhibited.

I pound her harder, holding her tight, groaning into her with every movement. My body tenses as my climax builds. I can't think straight. Nothing else exists but my cock thrusting into Emma, hard and fast. Electricity races through me, and my blood burns in my veins.

Her pussy tightens around me. She's getting hotter; I can feel how close she is to coming.

"Fuck, yes, Hunter, right there," she says.

I crush my mouth against hers, sliding my tongue in. I want to taste her, feel her, smell her. I fuck her in a steady rhythm, my balls tightening.

"Come in me," she says, her voice a whimper.

A hint of reason finds its way into my mind, and I realize I'm fucking her without a condom. It's a little late now, but I can hold back. "Ems, we aren't using protection."

"It's fine," she says. Her arms clutch around my neck and she rocks her hips into me. "I'm on the pill. Come in me, Hunter. I want to feel you come."

"I'm going to come in you so hard," I say. Clarity starts to come back, and I can think. I want her to come first. I don't want to miss her. "Come all over me, Ems. You feel so fucking good."

"Don't stop that," she says. "Oh, fuck, yes."

I slide in and out, pushing my cock deep inside her, giving her what she wants. Her heat builds and I barely hold myself in check.

She throws her head back and moans, her pussy clenching tight around me. One more thrust and I'm done for. I burst, filling her. My cock pulses in a mad rush, my body going stiff. I hold her ass, pushing my cock in hard as

I come, relishing the feel of her tight pussy surrounding me.

We're both breathing hard as we come down from the rush. Emma wraps her arms around my neck. I pull out and carefully lower her so her feet are on the floor. She doesn't let go, and I hold her, sliding my arms around her back.

I don't know what happens next, but right now, she's mine.

## 14

## EMMA

*I*'m breathing hard, and not quite sure what just happened—but I think Hunter fucked me senseless against his front door.

His arms hold me so tight, and I melt into him. God, that felt good. I love how he unleashed on me. During all the time we've spent together, he's been so careful. So controlled. Seeing the raw, aggressive side of him was incredible.

He pulls back and touches my face. His hand is so gentle. His lips press against mine, his tongue gently caressing my mouth. I open for him and he deepens his kiss, slow and luxurious. My mind is fuzzy, like I've had too much wine.

With his mouth still on mine, he leads me into his house. We get through his bedroom door and his hands slide around my back, finding the zipper on my dress. It slips to the floor and he unhooks my bra. He slides his fingers along my shoulders, pulling down the straps, and kisses along my collarbone.

I glance down and—holy shit—he's hard again already.

He runs his fingers through my hair. "God, Emma, I'll never get enough of you."

We move to his bed and he lays me down on my back. His eyes are so intense, drinking me in like he's never seen me before. Like he never expected to see me again. He moves his hand down and brushes my nipple with his fingers. I shiver at his touch, a thrill running through me.

He keeps exploring with his hands, lightly caressing my skin, planting soft kisses along the trail he follows. He lingers on my breasts, his tongue sliding along the hard nub of my nipple. I feel like I'm floating. His hand moves down to my thighs and he nudges my legs apart. My eyes roll back and I moan as he finds my clit, teasing it softly. He rubs harder, and it's like my body moves of its own accord. My hips rock up and down with his motion, his soft touch just what I need to come alive again.

"I love the way you touch me," I say, my voice breathy.

He smiles and kisses my mouth, his fingers working their magic. "I love the way you feel."

His hand stops and I gasp, but he climbs on top of me. His muscles are taut, glistening with a light sheen of sweat, his tattoos the sexiest thing I've ever seen. He has more on his chest, and I want to run my tongue along their lines.

He leans his forehead against mine. "You're so beautiful."

My eyes tear up, but before I can think about what's happening, he slides inside me again. His thickness stretches me open, filling me. It's bliss.

He moves in and out, with more gentleness this time, but every thrust has me heating up. His weight on top of me feels so fucking good. He kisses my neck and nibbles at my skin. I'm overcome, every sensation stirring something deep inside. Something I buried a long time ago.

"Harder." I dig my fingers into his back. "Harder, Hunter. I want more."

He picks up the pace, thrusting with more force. Our bodies surge and flow, locked together, moving in effortless unity. It's like we were made to fit together. So perfect. So right. He thrusts his hips, driving his cock in deep.

I'm overwhelmed, lost in the feel of his body, his skin on mine. I don't want him to stop. With him inside me, I don't have to think about what this means. The past is gone, and the future doesn't matter. The only thing that exists is us, in this moment. The feel of his cock, sliding in and out, every thrust bringing me closer to climax. His mouth on my skin, leaving searing hot marks where he kisses me. The strength of his arms, his muscular frame, poised above me. Everything else fades away.

"Fuck, Ems, I could do this forever," he says. "You feel amazing."

"Don't stop," I say. "I don't want this to end."

He keeps going, and we both move faster. We can't help it; surges of pleasure drive us onward. I can't remember the last time I had two orgasms so close together, and the sudden tension takes me by surprise. My core muscles clench, deep inside, driving me toward climax. I chase the feeling, grinding against Hunter with each thrust.

"Baby, I'm going to come," he says. His voice is deep and rough. He moves faster, and I love the feeling of him letting go of his tight control.

Without warning, he fucks me hard. His cock moves fast and I arch my back, clutching the sheets. My orgasm overtakes me, sends me spinning through nothingness until I'm so dizzy, I don't know which way is up. His cock pulses; his hot come fills me.

He pauses for a long moment, his cock still inside me,

his breath hot on my neck. He kisses beneath my ear, up my cheek, finds my lips. Then he rolls off me and pulls me into his arms. I rest my head on his shoulder and drape my arm across his chest as he kisses my hair and rubs slow circles along my arm.

My body is warm, thrumming with contentment. Hunter's chest rises and falls against me in a slow rhythm. I think he might have fallen asleep, but I can't be sure. A part of me hopes we both drift off and don't wake until morning. I'd rather feel like things just happened, almost outside of my control, than make a decision. Do I want to stay over? It felt so good to be with him again—to feel his hardness inside me, feel the pulses as he emptied into me. It was unlike anything I've ever had before, even with him. But now that I'm thinking about it, sleeping here feels like too much.

As good as that was, I'm worried I just made a very big mistake.

There was a time I thought I knew everything about him. He shared a side of himself with me that he never let anyone else see. It made me feel special, like I'd unlocked a secret no one else knew. People saw him as sullen and easily enraged; I knew the Hunter who was gentle and sweet.

But there was always something else in his eyes—even in our quietest, most tender moments. Rage. But I don't see it anymore.

Except that when he slammed Wyatt onto the hood of his car, I saw it burning hot.

I was so shocked when Wyatt grabbed me. He's never laid a hand on me in anger before. He knew how to push my buttons and say things to get under my skin, but he never tried to hurt me. I don't know what he would have done if Hunter hadn't been there, but the speed and ferocity with which Hunter reacted scared the shit out of me. I was more than a little convinced Hunter was going to break his arm. Or worse.

Where is Hunter hiding that rage now? How did he unleash it so fast?

What else might set him off?

I'm in too deep and I'm not quite sure how I got here. Just a few weeks ago, I was happily done with men. I wanted to be single, to work on recapturing the woman I used to be. The woman I should be.

Hunter's arm tightens around me and he kisses my head.

I squeeze my eyes shut. I'm so confused. My body wants to melt into him.

"Ems?" Hunter's voice is quiet.

"Yeah?"

He kisses my forehead again. "Are you all right?"

I close my eyes against the sting of tears. The first time we made love he asked me that same question, in that same gentle voice. "I don't know."

He lifts his head off the pillow to look me in the eyes. He touches the side of my face with his strong hand. "I want you to stay with me tonight." His lips touch mine in a soft kiss and he runs his hand through my hair.

My body relaxes as his kiss deepens. He feels so right. Why am I fighting this? I slide my hand up his chest.

He pulls away just enough that our lips part, our noses still touching. "Will you stay?" he whispers.

I meet his gaze. "Yes. I'll stay."

He smiles and kisses me again.

I want to believe I'm doing the right thing, but I'm still not sure.

～

Loud banging jolts me from sleep. I'm lying on my side, my head on the pillow, and it takes me a second to remember where I am.

Hunter is already sitting up, as if he woke instantly.

"It's okay, it's just someone knocking on the door," he says.

I glance at the time on his bedside clock. It's just after eight.

The sheet slides off Hunter as he gets out of bed, showing off his very hot ass. He quickly pulls on a pair of underwear and tugs on some jeans and a white t-shirt.

Someone knocks again.

He leans down and kisses me lightly on the mouth. "You don't have to get up. I'll see who it is."

I decide to put my clothes back on. All I have is my dress from last night, but I feel awkward lying here naked. Who could be here?

It better not be Wyatt. I don't know what Hunter would do to him.

I put on my dress and step out into the hallway. I hear voices from the front of the house.

"I'm sorry, Hunter, but I have to ask you to come in so we can ask you a few questions."

"Am I under arrest?"

Arrest? What the hell? I tiptoe closer and peek around the wall.

Two cops in uniform are standing outside the door. I can just see them past Hunter's large frame.

"No, you're not under arrest," one of the cops says. "But we have a report we need to follow up on. Will you come with me, please?"

Hunter's shoulders move as he takes a deep breath. "Okay. Will you give me a minute, officers?"

He turns and I shrink back into the hallway, my heart racing. He takes my arm and leads me back to his bedroom.

"What's going on?" I ask in a low voice.

"I think your ex called the police last night and reported that I attacked him."

"Attacked him?" I say. "No, he grabbed me, and—"

Hunter puts a finger to my lips. "I know. It's okay. I'll go in and tell them what happened. I'm sure it won't take very long."

"I'll come, too," I say. "I'm sure I can clear this up."

"No," he says. "I don't want you to have to do that."

"Don't you think they'll want to hear from me?"

He touches the side of my face. "Ems, please. You've been through enough. I can take care of this." He kisses me, his mouth firm against mine. "I'll be back in a little while."

He leaves out the front door before I can protest.

## 15

## HUNTER

*I* could really use some coffee, but I have a feeling the stuff they have sitting in the coffee pot on the counter is shit. The officers have been polite—almost apologetic—and I know they're just doing their job. The fact that Emma's douche of an ex called them makes me hope I never fucking see him again. Because next time they'll be bringing me in for more than questions. I'll find myself handcuffed and tossed in a cell.

It would be worth it.

I keep my face pleasant and relaxed, despite the hum of anger buzzing through me. Officer Cooper knows me, but the rest of them don't, and I don't want to appear threatening. That's harder than it sounds. I'm aware of how I look. I'm a big guy, my arms are tatted up, and I still have my military posture. I look like a fucking Marine, and I'm goddamn proud of it.

I also know I have an arsenal of weapons at my property —all properly licensed and legal, but not the sort of thing most people keep on hand. I have every clearance I need, and I can flood this small town police station with paperwork proving I have a right to do what I do. But that kind of scrutiny would be a hassle, and I don't need that.

Emma looked horrified when the cops showed up. I'm glad they didn't ask if she was there. I know she could clear things up pretty quickly by explaining her side of the story, but I absolutely do not want her to have to talk to the police. I want to take care of this for her so she can stop thinking about that jackass.

I just hope she isn't scared of me after seeing me manhandle him last night. She has no reason to fear me, but I'm not sure how to prove it. Time, I suppose, like everything else. I'll bury anyone who tries to hurt her, but I'd never lay a finger on her.

Not in anger, anyway. When it comes to Emma, I'd like to do lots of things with my fingers. And my tongue. And my cock.

I clear my throat and shift in my chair. I need to quit that line of thinking right now, or things are going to get awkward.

Officer Cooper sits down across the desk from me.

"Okay, Hunter," he says. "I just need to ask you a few questions."

"Sure."

He thumbs through some papers. "The person who made the report against you claims you attacked him without provocation. He says you grabbed his arm, almost breaking it, and slammed his head into the hood of a parked car. He goes on to say you threatened to kill him."

Interesting. Not exactly lies, but not quite the whole truth, either.

"That's partially correct," I say.

Cooper raises his eyebrows at me. "Partially? Which part?"

"Bits and pieces," I say. "Did he mention the part about me being on a date with his ex-wife?"

Cooper's eyes dart back and forth over the page. "No, he did not mention that."

"The person in question wanted to talk to my date. She agreed. I gave them space to talk. They argued, and she tried to extricate herself from the situation. He acted aggressively, grabbing her arm, and attempted to restrain her. I made sure he couldn't."

"And by that you mean..."

"I put him in a non-lethal submission hold until he agreed to leave."

"Did you slam his head into a car?" Cooper asks.

"I did not," I say. "The submission hold did include the use of the hood of his own car, but his head did not slam against it."

"And did you threaten to kill him?" he asks.

I pause. Technically, I didn't threaten to kill him. "I did not."

"So, he made that up out of nowhere?" Cooper asks.

"I may have indicated that, as a Marine, I've been in a position that required the use of lethal force," I say. "The rest he inferred on his own. But I did *not* say I would kill him."

Cooper leans back in his chair and pauses, looking over his paperwork again. "Well, I don't think there's anything we need to charge you with. The alleged victim isn't injured, so I can't say you used excessive force on him. And you mouthing off to your date's ex-husband isn't a crime, especially if he was mouthing off to her first. Even less so if he got physical with her."

I give him a closed mouth smile, but let him do the talking.

"I think you scared this guy, and he thought he could make trouble for you," Cooper says.

"Sounds like it," I say. "Unfortunately for him, the only trouble he's really caused is making me late for breakfast."

Cooper smiles. "All right, Hunter, you're free to go. Do you need a ride or anything?"

"No, I'll call someone," I say. I don't particularly want to ride in a police car again.

I stand and Cooper follows. He holds out his hand and I shake it.

"Sorry for the inconvenience," he says.

"It's no problem," I say. "You need to do your job. I respect that."

I leave out the front door and debate who to call. I don't want to make Emma come get me. She doesn't have her car at my place, and I'm not sure if she'd be comfortable coming to get me in my truck. Plus, what do I say? *Hi Emma, thanks for the awesome sex last night, but can you come pick me up at the police station now?*

My folks are a *hell no*. I am not explaining this to Mom. One of my brothers is probably the obvious choice. Ryan will be less likely to lecture me than Cody, but he lives farther away.

Then it occurs to me. Clover.

I text her. *Hey almost-sister. I had a little mishap and I need you to bust me out of the police station. Do NOT tell Cody.*

Her reply is almost immediate. *I've got your back, bro. Tell me what to do.*

She is so funny. *I'll handle getting outside. I need you to drive getaway. Five minutes.*

*Done.*

She's here in less than five minutes, but she looks disappointed when she pulls up and sees me outside. "Hey," she says, flashing a smile. "You're not being very covert, standing out here in broad daylight."

"Oh, I took care of everyone inside already." I walk around and get in her passenger side. "They'll all be fine, but they can expect some wicked headaches after the ass kicking I just gave them."

She laughs. "Say, do you mind if I go in for a minute? I want to ask if one of them will give me a pair of handcuffs."

I roll my eyes. "Oh god, Clover, gross. Cody's my brother."

She giggles. "Whatever. You don't even know the half of it."

"I do not want to know," I say. "But I don't think they'll give you handcuffs."

"Fine," she says. "What happened, anyway? You get caught jacking off in the movie theater or something?"

I shake my head and laugh. "No. I did arm bar Emma's ex, though."

She turns to me with a wicked grin. "This I have to hear."

I tell her about our run-in with Wyatt, not bothering with the careful word choices I used with Officer Cooper. I just tell her straight-up what happened.

"That's fantastic," she says. "And hey, a date with Emma? That's awesome."

"Yeah, it was," I say. "Very awesome."

"What happened afterward?" she asks.

I try not to smile, but I can't help it.

"Bow chicka bow wow," she says. "Hunter got lucky!"

"Shut up, weirdo."

Clover laughs. "No, seriously, that's so great. I'm glad things are working out after that rough start. You guys getting married yet?"

"No," I say. "Not even close. Last night was ... fuck, it was amazing. But she's pretty convinced she doesn't want a relationship. I think I'm getting to her, but it's going to take a while."

"It's too bad she's so closed off to the potential," she says.

I shrug. "She's been burned pretty bad. Twice. Once by me."

"True," she says. "That's a lot to get past, I guess."

"It is," I say. "I just need to give her time."

"Are you good at oral?" Clover asks. "Because that will definitely help."

"That was a completely serious question, wasn't it?"

She looks at me like I'm crazy. "Of course it was. So, are you?"

I laugh again. How am I having this conversation with my brother's fiancée? "Yeah, that's not an issue."

"Like, legitimately good, or you just think you are?" she asks. "Because there's a big difference."

"Seriously, Clover, it's called a filter."

"I'm just saying. So, am I taking you home?"

"Yeah," I say. "Thanks for the ride."

"I'll drive getaway any time."

Clover drops me off, and I go inside to find Emma sitting at the kitchen table. She looks sexy as hell in one of my t-shirts and a pair of my boxers. I could really get used to this.

"Oh god, Hunter, what happened?" she says as she stands up.

For half a second, I'm unsure about touching her. Last night we were both amped up after what happened at the bar, and I know that had a lot to do with her willingness to sleep with me. But my gut tells me that now is the time to try pushing past her walls a little more.

I smile at her, stepping close, and kiss her before I

answer. "It was fine, really. Once they heard what happened, they apologized for wasting my time and sent me on my way."

"I am so sorry," she says. "I still can't believe he called the police."

"It's not your fault."

She glances down at her clothes—or my clothes, rather. They're too big on her, but I love how unkempt she looks.

"Sorry, I didn't have anything else to wear," she says. "And you sort of tore my panties last night."

Oh, shit, I did tear them off her, didn't I? "Yeah, sorry about that." I slip my hand around her waist and draw her closer. "I like you in my shirt, though."

"Yeah?"

I move my hands to her hips and pull her against me. She doesn't resist. I'm hard again. Her body is intoxicating. I lean my mouth close to her ear. "You look sexy as hell, Emma. Like I fucked you good last night—and maybe you want me to do it again."

I kiss down her neck and she leans her head back, a soft moan escaping her lips.

"Hunter, I don't know…"

I slip my hands beneath the waistband of the boxers and grab her ass. "Do you want me to stop?" I kiss just behind her ear and she shudders.

"No."

"Are you sure?" I ask.

"I'm sure."

I find her mouth and kiss her—soft at first. Her lips part for me and I feel her tongue brush against mine. A surge of desire floods me and I grab the back of her head, deepening the kiss. She unbuttons my jeans and reaches in to grab my very hard cock.

The bed is too damn far away, so I pull her to the couch. We stop kissing long enough to lift off our shirts, then I touch her face and kiss her again. She holds my arms, digging in her fingers.

I ease her down onto her back. What Clover said runs through my mind. *Are you good at oral? Because that will definitely help.*

I lick my lips and pull off the boxers. "I like you in my clothes, but I like you even more like this."

Emma laughs. I start at her knee, kissing my way up her thigh. I reach her center and taste her, just above her opening.

She sucks in a quick breath. "Oh, Hunter."

I flick her clit with my tongue a few times. "This is something we haven't done before, isn't it?"

"No, I don't think we have," she says, her voice breathy.

I tease my tongue in a slow circle around her clit, and she shudders. Fuck, she tastes good. I slip my tongue into her pussy and run it up and down, in and out, pressing against her clit. She writhes, tilting her hips into me.

"Oh, fuck, Hunter, how are you doing that?"

I grab her ass and massage her clit with my tongue. I find a rhythm she seems to like and don't let up. God, I love making her feel good. She moans and lifts her arms over her head, arching her back.

I desperately want my cock inside her, but I have to make her come like this. I want my mouth on her hot pussy when she unleashes. I pick up the pace and feel her respond. She calls out and I know I have her. I push my tongue inside her, sucking on her clit again, and her pussy throbs. She runs her hands through my hair, rocking her hips into me, calling my name as she comes.

I kiss my way down her thighs while she catches her

breath. I'm burning with the need to be inside her; my cock is so hard it hurts.

"That was amazing," she says between breaths.

"You taste so good, I could do that to you every day." I sit on the couch and she climbs on top of me, straddling my lap.

"Do you want more of me?" she asks, holding herself just above my tip.

"Fuck, yes." I grab her hips, but she resists, teasing me with her wet folds.

She settles onto me slowly, inch by inch. I groan and lean my head back. Fuck, she's so good. Her pussy is so wet, I slide right in. She grinds up against me a few times, pushing me in deeper.

With my hands on her hips, I rock her back and forth. She arches her back and I take her nipple in my mouth, sucking gently. I love the way she feels; I love every bit of her. Her blond hair spills down her back as she tilts her head, moaning as she rides me.

I'm already so amped up from tasting her sweet pussy, I'm close to coming. She leans her forehead against mine, meeting my eyes. It's like she knows. She feels my climax building and moves slower to stretch out the bliss.

But I need more. I dig my fingers into her ass and move her faster, thrusting into her with every stroke. She calls out, uninhibited, the sound of her pleasure urging me on.

Her pussy tightens, pulsing around me, and she threads her fingers through my hair. My own orgasm tears through me, hitting me in waves. It's so intense, my adrenaline spikes, and the orgasm goes on and on.

When I finally finish, I'm breathing hard. Emma collapses against me, and I put my arms around her to keep her close. I know I have to take her home soon. I have to work later, and she probably does, too. But being inside her again was better than I could have imagined. Nothing in my memory prepared me for the way she would make me feel.

I want to tell her. I want her to know everything I feel for her. How much I want her, that I would do anything—risk anything—to have her. But I can't find the words. I'm afraid of scaring her away, so I just hold her, stroking her soft skin.

For now, this will have to be enough.

## 16

---

## EMMA

*H*unter drops me off at home later that day, and I'm very grateful that Gabe is such a workaholic. I doubt he even noticed I didn't come back last night. I don't want to have to explain things to him. Not yet.

I shower and put on clean clothes, trying not to think about how much I already miss Hunter. I can't deny how good it felt to be with him again. He was incredible— touching me like he *knew*. I was completely swept away by his body, his kisses, the power of him inside me. Even our date was fantastic. We laughed and talked with such ease. With Wyatt, I would have been tense the whole time, worried about whether his dinner would come out wrong and ruin his mood. Or afraid to say something that would make him suspect I was working behind his back. God, what a fucked-up relationship that was. I want to kick myself for putting up with it for so long.

But Hunter was not only a perfect gentleman, he made me feel like I could be myself. And with where I am in my life right now, that's priceless.

Bonus points for the way he used his tongue this morning. That was fucking fantastic.

I check my phone and smile when I see I have a text from my old friend Ashlyn. She and I used to be super close, but I lost touch with her after I married Wyatt. I reached out to her on Facebook and we've been trying to make plans to get together. She's available for lunch, so I decide to go for it.

We agree to meet at Old Town Cafe. I pull up in front of the restaurant and my phone vibrates with a text. It's from Hunter, and I bite my lip.

*Is it bad that I miss you?*

Oh god, Hunter. How does he know exactly what to say to make my tummy flutter? I didn't think I was capable of feeling that way anymore.

I send a reply. *If it is, then I'm just as naughty.*

*You can be naughty for me anytime.*

I giggle and glance at the time. Ashlyn is probably here already. I should go inside, but I get another text.

*When can I see you again?*

I blow out a breath. I need to be careful. I'm afraid to let my guard down. What should I say? Friday? It's only Monday, and I don't really want to wait that long. I don't want to wait at all, but I'm getting way ahead of myself.

*This is Hunter, Emma.* Tongue savvy aside, I should keep him at a distance. Take it slow.

But fuck, his tongue. It was very convincing.

*I'm free anytime. Tomorrow?*

*I'll wait that long if you make me, but no promises.*

I smile again and put my phone in my purse. I go inside and find Ashlyn sitting at a table near the front counter. She waves when I walk in the door, a big smile crossing her face. The tips of her wavy blond hair are dyed pink and she's wearing a loose black tank top with an arrow and the words *Go My Own Way* printed on it. Yep, that's Ashlyn.

"Emma!"

She stands up to hug me, and suddenly I'm choked up. Ashlyn and I were inseparable in high school. We stayed friends in college, and she was my maid of honor when I got married. It's been at least five years since I've seen her and I can't believe how much I've missed her.

I swipe my fingers under my eyes. "It's so great to see you."

"Aw, Emma, are you getting teary on me?" she says. "You need to quit it or we're both going to cry."

We sit down and I take a deep breath. "I know, I'm sorry. I just haven't seen you in so long. You look amazing."

"Thanks," she says. "So do you. Better than last time I saw you. Losing a hundred seventy pounds looks good on you."

I laugh. She never liked Wyatt. "Isn't that the truth. I just want to say, for the record, I should have listened to you instead of my mother. You were right about him."

"Honestly? It sucks being right," she says. "I wish I'd been wrong. So, tell me what happened."

I shrug. "He was so hard to live with. He didn't like his job, so he'd come home grumpy. But he didn't want me to work, so I couldn't even contribute and make things easier financially."

"What kind of messed-up crap is that?" Ashlyn asks.

"I know," I say. "Nothing was ever good enough. I think he wanted some kind of perfect housewife who would keep his house sparkling clean and make gourmet meals and have lots of babies. I was always pretending, trying to figure out who he wanted me to be. I got sick of it."

"I'm really proud of you for leaving," Ashlyn says. "I

wish you would have gotten in touch sooner, though. I could have helped you out."

"I'm sorry," I say. "I should have. I feel like I lost so much of who I am when I was with him. I pulled away from all my friends, even my family. I thought about calling you, but I wasn't sure if you'd want to see me."

Ashlyn raises an eyebrow. "You really think some jackass would get between us forever? Come on. Of course I want to see you. I'm not trying to make you feel guilty, so knock that off. I let things slide as much as you did. It's not like I tried very hard to keep in touch over the last few years. So, the divorce is final, right?"

"Yes, although it took forever," I say. "He fought me on everything."

"What a dick," she says. "It's a good thing you guys never had kids."

I groan. "Can you imagine? He was pushing hard for kids, too. He got mad every time he saw tampons in the bathroom."

"How did you avoid it?"

"I've actually never told anyone, but I went on birth control behind his back. I paid cash at a clinic so he wouldn't find out."

"It's so messed up that you had to do that," she says. "Has he left you alone since the divorce?"

"Not really," I say. "He did for a while, but he left a note on my apartment door right before I moved out. And then he showed up out here Saturday night."

"Are you serious?" she says, leaning forward. "What happened?"

"Holy shit, it was intense. I was out with someone, and we went to Danny's for a drink. Wyatt was there, sitting at the bar. We tried to leave, but he saw me. He said he just wanted to talk. I figured I better just talk to him so he'd leave me alone."

"What did he want?" she asks.

"I don't know, he kept saying he wanted to know what went wrong," I say. "I don't know what I'm supposed to tell him. I think he's just pissed because I left him. It hurt his ego. So we were standing there talking, and I tried to walk away and he grabbed my arm. And then Hunter grabbed him and—"

"Woah," Ashlyn says, putting a hand up. "Stop right there. Did you just say what I think you said, or are you talking about someone else named Hunter?"

I pause, my mouth half open. "Um, no I mean Hunter. Hunter Evans."

Ashlyn sits back in her chair. "You were out with Hunter?"

"Yes."

"Hunter Evans? *The* Hunter Evans? Big guy, kind of a mean face, but still strangely hot? The one who ripped your heart to shreds?"

"Yes, that Hunter Evans."

"Holy shit, Emma," she says, her voice quiet.

"I know," I say. "I *really* know."

"Oh my god, that *was* him," she says. "I've seen a guy that looks like him around town, but I figured I had to be imagining things. How is it you were out with Hunter?"

"Well, he moved back last year, I guess. I ran into him at Charlie's one day, and I kind of told him off and left."

Ashlyn crosses her arms. "Good. He deserved it."

"Yeah, he did," I say. "But then later he invited me to coffee, and I figured I might as well. I've been wondering what happened to him all this time, and seeing him again ... it was so confusing. After that, he wouldn't let up. He kept asking to hang out, and it was really hard to say no. Eventually I agreed to go on an actual date with him."

"But Emma, it's Hunter. You guys were like, on the brink of getting married too young, and then he totally bailed. He disappeared. It was awful."

"Believe me, I know." I hate reliving those memories. "It *was* awful. I didn't think I'd ever get over it. And I know this makes me sound like an idiot, but he's so different now. That mean face thing? He doesn't have it anymore. I saw it for a second when he slammed Wyatt into the hood of his car, but the rest of the time, he's so relaxed and easy going."

"He slammed Wyatt into the hood of a car?" Ashlyn says with a laugh. "Okay, that earns him a few points."

I smile. "It was ... damn it, Ash, it was hot. It was kind of scary, and it should not have been a turn-on."

"But it was?"

A little jolt of electricity runs through me at the memory and I shift in my seat. "Yeah, it really was. He um, he took me back to his place after."

"Damn, Emma." Ashlyn raises her eyebrows and leans forward. "Okay, was it good?"

"It was ... amazing," I say. "I don't think I've ever had sex that good. I'm talking mind-blowing."

"That's another point in his favor," she says. "Or, ten points. So, what, are you guys back together now?"

"No," I say, emphatic. "We are not back together. I'm not interested in a serious relationship right now, and he knows that. I've made myself very clear."

"Friends with benefits is fun," Ashlyn says. "Although, I'm just going to be honest: I don't know how you do friends with benefits with your ex-boyfriend. Or with a guy who obviously wasn't just trying to get in your pants."

"How do you know he *wasn't* just trying to get in my pants?"

"I guess I don't," Ashlyn says. "But how hard is a guy really going to work for that? I'm sure your kitty purrs real nice, but how long did he have to pursue you before he got you in bed?"

"Yeah, we did hang out a lot before that happened," I say. "I told him a million times I didn't want a relationship, and he kept saying it was fine, we could just be friends."

"Right, I'm sure that's all he wanted," Ashlyn says, raising an eyebrow.

"What does that mean?" I ask. "A second ago you said he wouldn't have put in so much effort if he was only trying to get in my pants."

"No, I don't think he was only out to get laid," she says. "Well, of course he wanted that. You're hot as hell, most guys want in your pants. But that whole *we're just friends* thing? He's gunning for adding the word *girl* in front of *friend*."

"You haven't seen him in ten years, and you have him all figured out?"

"Not at all," she says. "In fact, I have way more questions about him than answers. But the fact that he's into you, and wants to be more than a hookup for old time's sake, is pretty obvious, even from way over here."

I sigh. "Can't I just ... hang out with him sometimes and have toe-curling sex, and just leave it at that?"

"God, you're a dream for every guy who fears commitment," she says. "Speaking from experience, that kind of setup works best when there aren't a bunch of big feels between you, and when both people are clear about what they want. And even then, it can wind up complicated pretty quickly. And you two are already complicated."

"I know. I feel like maybe I've gotten myself in over my

head, here. I swore off men completely, and then in walks Hunter."

"Swearing off men is a terrible idea anyway," she says with a wave of her hand.

"Of course you would think that. What about you?" I ask. I want to change the subject. "You're not married. Are you with someone?"

"Kind of?" she says, like she's not sure. "I don't know, he lives an hour away, which is a pain. But he's amazing in bed, so there's that."

I laugh. "There is that. I guess you're still a man-eater."

She shrugs. "I like men. Sue me. Although it wouldn't be terrible to find the right one someday. I just don't know if that's possible for me. I get bored too easily."

"It would take a pretty special guy to tame you." I pause. "Ash, it's so good to hang out again. I haven't had anyone to talk to like this in such a long time."

Ashlyn smiles. "It's awesome having you back. I'll even forgive you for not letting me help you leave that dickface. Damn it, Emma, we could have had a kick-ass divorce party."

I think back on my sad little champagne and cheesecake for one. "Yeah, I really missed out. All I did was eat cheesecake."

"That isn't a bad start. But we'll have to do better at some point," she says. "But Emma? Be careful with Hunter. I know it's been a long time, but that whole thing was really messed up. I don't want to see you get hurt like that again."

"I'll be careful," I say. "Promise. And can we do this again sometime?"

"We better," she says. "You need your girl time."

"I really do." I start feeling teary again, so I take a deep breath. "Thanks, Ashlyn."

We finish our coffee, catching up on the last several years. I'm amazed at how easily we can talk, as if no time has passed at all. Hanging out with Ashlyn makes me feel more like myself than I have in a long time.

Project Get Emma Back is in full swing.

## 17

# EMMA

*I* know Ashlyn is right—I need to be careful with Hunter. But he's making it very, very hard.

He finds compelling reasons for us to get together all the time. At first, he asks me out on proper dates. There's almost a formality to it—he has a destination in mind, whether it's dinner, or a movie, or even just an afternoon coffee. He calls or texts to ask, picks me up, and we go out. Of course, we often end up back at his place. The crazy thing is, I never feel like he expects it. If a date wound down and I asked him to take me home, I'm sure he would do it without complaint.

But I never want him to.

After a few weeks, I notice a change. Instead of always asking me to go out with him somewhere, he starts inviting me over to his house, just to hang out. Sometimes he surprises me by stopping by with coffee. On a Friday afternoon, he comes over with a box of fresh vegetables from his mom's garden and makes us dinner. We spend time together casually, whenever we're both free.

I realize this has crossed the line from *maybe I'll go on a date with you* to *I am definitely dating you*.

But that's fine. We can date casually. There's nothing wrong with seeing someone you like, especially when there's so much chemistry. And our chemistry is off the charts. It always was. I've been completely honest with Hunter about how I feel and what I want. I'm okay with dating ... but this is not serious. I can back out anytime.

Gabe looks pretty skeptical when I tell him I'm seeing Hunter. Despite the fact that I assure him it's just a casual thing, he tells me multiple times that I should be careful. I also face seeing my mother, and let her know Hunter is back in town. She's much more of a grudge holder than Gabe, especially since my father left her. She wastes no time telling me what a terrible idea it is to see him again, regardless of whether or not it's serious. I keep my mouth shut tight while she gets it out of her system. I understand her concerns, and I tell her I'm not in a place in my life where I want a long-term relationship anyway, so she has nothing to worry about.

Of course, being with Hunter feels as easy and natural as breathing, and the more time we spend together, the more I wonder if I'm kidding myself about not being serious about him. But I squash that thought whenever it pops into my head. We have fun together, the sex is unbelievable, and that's enough for now.

On a Friday afternoon, I get a text from Hunter. I haven't been able to see him in a couple days, and my heart does a little leap when I see his name on my phone.

*Hey Ems, mind if I stop by?*

I smile and text back. *Not at all. See you in a few.*

In less than ten minutes, there's a knock at my door. Hunter pulls me in for a kiss as soon as I answer. His lips are soft against mine and I relax into him.

"Hi," he says. "It's so good to see you."

I smile and kiss him again. "Come in."

He follows me inside, and we both head over to the couch to sit down.

"So what's up?"

"Something came up this weekend, kind of last minute, but I was wondering if you might want to come," he says.

"Come, where?" I ask.

"Camping," he says. "My brothers are going and they've been bugging me to come with them. I wasn't going to, but then I thought it might be fun for us to go. You know, together. Nicole and Clover will be there, so the testosterone shouldn't be totally unbearable."

"I haven't been camping in years," I say.

"Really?" he says, drawing his eyebrows together. "You used to love camping. That's why I thought I'd invite you."

"I know," I say. "It was my favorite, but..."

Hunter nods. I don't even need to say why.

He takes a deep breath and I can tell there's something else. "So, Ems, I haven't really talked to my family about us yet. It's not that I don't want to; I do. I felt like I needed to keep this protective bubble around us, and if I started telling people that you and I were seeing each other again, I might jinx it."

"Oh, that's okay," I say. "We're not so serious that I'd expect you to tell your family."

His expression darkens and he glances away for a moment. "Right, yeah. Of course not. So, I guess my point is, if camping with my brothers is too much for you, I understand. But I also thought it could be fun. I'd like to go, but I don't really want to without you."

I pause. Camping does sound like fun, and I certainly don't hate the idea of camping with Hunter. We used to go camping and hiking together all the time.

"You know what? I'd love to."

"Yeah?"

"Definitely," I say. "I miss camping. Where are we going?"

"There's a campground up north on the peninsula that we go to a lot."

"I literally have no camping gear," I say. "I doubt Gabe does either. He's not really the camping type."

"That's okay, I have everything," he says. "Just pack some clothes. I'll take care of the rest."

"When are we leaving?"

He shrugs. "Whenever you can. Everyone else left this morning, so they'll be there by the time we get there. If you have to work, I can come back and pick you up later."

"No, I can be done for the day," I say.

"Okay, great."

I pack a bag, trying to remember what I'll need for camping. Then I send Gabe a quick text, letting him know I'll be gone for the weekend.

We hop in Hunter's truck, and after a stop at his place to get his camping gear, we head north. It's about a two-hour drive to the campground. We listen to music and chat, and it goes by quickly. Hunter's brothers already have the campsite set up when we arrive. It's secluded among tall fir trees, and they have a fire going. Two tents are set up and there's room for another on the far side.

Ryan raises a beer in greeting as Hunter pulls up. Nicole and Clover are sitting in camping chairs around the fire, and Cody is standing nearby.

I get out of the car and Clover jumps out of her seat, squealing.

"Emma! Holy shit, you brought Emma! Hunter, you didn't tell us!"

I remember Clover from the first time I saw Hunter. She has curly blond hair and she's dressed in a pair of jean shorts and a t-shirt. She walks toward me with a huge smile on her face.

"Hi!" she says. "We met before, but it was a little weird because I was kind of stalking you. I'm Clover."

I notice Ryan give Cody a confused look, but Cody just shrugs.

"Hi," I say. "I'm glad you did that, I guess?"

She purses her lips and looks at Hunter. "Told you."

I wave at Ryan and Cody. "Hi, guys."

I walk over to the fire and Ryan hands me a beer. "Hey, Emma. Been a long time." He looks over at Hunter with one eyebrow raised. "It's cool you guys could make it."

"Thanks."

"You can hang out here," Hunter says. "I'll unload our stuff."

Nicole unfolds another camping chair and sets it next to her while Hunter walks back to his truck. I remember Nicole from high school, but we didn't know each other very well. She has dark blond hair that hangs just past her collarbone, and she's wearing a red hoodie and shorts.

"Hey," Nicole says as I take a seat next to her. "Sorry if we're all looking at you weird. Hunter has literally not said a word about you." She gasps and puts a hand to her mouth. "Oh god, that sounded so bad. I'm sorry. I didn't mean it like that. I just mean we didn't know you were coming."

"Yeah," Clover says as she sits down. "And you're like, the famous Emma, so this is kind of a big deal."

"I don't know about famous," I say.

"You're definitely Jacobsen family famous," Clover says. "You're the love of Hunter's life."

"Clover!" Nicole says.

"What?" Clover asks. "Like she doesn't know that already?"

Nicole turns back to me. "I'm sorry, Clover is, um…"

"It's okay, I get it," I say. "Hunter and I have a lot of history together."

"It's really sweet though," Nicole says. "I didn't realize you guys reconnected."

"Are you engaged yet?" Clover asks.

My mouth drops open.

Nicole smacks her on the arm. "Clover!"

"I'm sorry," Clover says. "I haven't eaten all day and Ryan keeps handing me beers."

I laugh. "No, Hunter and I … we're not really that serious or anything." I look up and realize Hunter is watching me. He adjusts his grip on the tent and walks past.

Cody comes up behind Clover and kisses the top of her head while he grabs the beer from her chair's drink holder. "I think you've had enough for now, sunshine."

"Do you think he needs help with that?" I ask, gesturing toward Hunter.

Nicole shrugs. "Ryan can help if he does."

"See?" Ryan says. He pokes a stick into the fire. "This is married life, Cody. She gets to volunteer me for everything."

"Oh, stop," Nicole says, smiling at him. "You love being married to me."

"Hell yeah, I love being married to you," Ryan says. He crouches in front of her and grabs the back of her neck, bringing her in for a kiss.

I realize I'm staring at them and I look away, taking a sip of my beer.

"Fuck, Ryan, you have a tent over there," Hunter calls out. "Go use it."

Ryan stands up and gives Hunter the finger. Nicole bites

her bottom lip, and her cheeks flush, but it looks pretty on her.

Hunter comes over to stand next to me and brushes his hands together. "I'm sorry, Ems. They're like that all the time. Hanging out with these four is like being at a fucking high school make-out party."

I laugh, particularly because while Hunter was talking, Clover stood up and started kissing Cody.

Hunter notices and rolls his eyes. "See?" He grabs a beer out of the cooler and pulls up a chair next to me.

"I guess I can see why you wanted to bring me along," I say. "You've been feeling left out."

"Yeah, a little bit. Mostly I just didn't want to be away from you." He smiles and holds up his beer. "To reconnecting."

I smile back and clink my bottle against his.

We hang out around the fire for a while, chatting. It's pleasantly warm with a light breeze blowing through the branches. Sitting around the fire was always my favorite part of camping. Time seems to slow down, without all the distractions of the world. Nicole and Clover are sweet and friendly. Hunter jokes around with his brothers. Any awkwardness I felt when we first arrived melts away as the afternoon goes on.

"So, what do you guys think? We have some daylight left. Anyone up for a short hike?" Cody asks. "Or should we save it for tomorrow?"

"Yeah, that sounds fun," Nicole says, and Ryan nods.

I glance at Hunter.

"You know what guys, I think I'll pass," Hunter says. "I don't think I'm up for it. Maybe tomorrow."

"You okay?" Ryan asks.

"Yeah, it's no big deal," Hunter says. "Busted leg aches today, but I'm fine."

"Keep the fire going, then," Cody says. "We won't be long."

The others head out, leaving me and Hunter by the fire. We sit quietly, staring into the flames.

After a while, I break the silence. "Can I ask you a question?"

"Sure."

"How did you get injured?"

He takes a deep breath, his eyes still on the fire. "I was overseas. I can't really tell you much about what I was doing. We were driving, and the vehicle in front of me hit an IED. I tried to swerve and miss it, but there wasn't anything I could do."

My stomach twists. "Oh god, Hunter. Are you serious?"

"Yeah," he says. "I don't remember much else, honestly. Except the noise. There was so much noise, and heat. I really thought I was going to die. After that, I have no idea what happened. I was out. I woke up in a hospital."

I stare at him. I can't imagine all the things he must have been through, the things he's seen. I put my hand on his arm. "I'm so sorry."

He puts a hand over mine. "It's okay. I lived. Some of them didn't."

"Is it hard?" I ask. "Coming home and being here again. You were gone a long time, and I sort of forget you were living such a different life."

"It was really hard at first," he says. "But it gets easier as time goes on. I had a lot of nightmares and stuff for a while. That wasn't fun. Ryan actually convinced me to talk to a therapist, so I did for about six months, and she really helped. I still get amped up sometimes and feel my control slipping, but I'm getting better. I know what to do now when I feel like I'm going to panic. I can usually cope with it."

"That's awful," I say. "I wish you didn't have to go through all that."

"There's a lot I wish I didn't have to see. Or do. But I did good things, too. More good than bad." His phone rings and he pulls it out of his pocket. His brow furrows. "I'm sorry, Ems, I need to take this."

He gets up and walks over by his truck. His limp is usually barely noticeable, but I can see him leaning heavily on his other leg.

His back is to me, and I can't help but wonder who he's talking to. Most of the time, he seems like an open book. But once in a while, I get the feeling there's something he's hiding. Or maybe I'm just looking for something to be wrong. For all I know, it's something about work. There's no reason I should be worried because he wants to take a quick phone call in private.

Is there?

I sigh and pick up a stick to poke at the fire.

He comes back after a few minutes, and I hope he'll tell me who it was. I don't want to ask—that feels too invasive—but it isn't the first time he's stepped away to take a call when we've been together.

"Sorry," he says.

"No problem."

I hate the little sliver of doubt that pricks my mind. I want to trust him, but it isn't that simple. There's a cloud hanging over the two of us, and I'm not sure we can ever get out from under it.

## 18

### HUNTER

*T*here's nothing quite like waking up next to Emma. I'm incapable of sleeping late anymore, but I love to wake up early and enjoy the feel of her sleeping quietly beside me. She doesn't stay over nearly as often as I'd like. Of course, I'd ask her to move in with me if I thought it would go over well, so nothing less than always is enough.

I hold her body close. She was cold when we went to bed, so we zipped our sleeping bags together and she curled up against me. The feel of her ass on my cock was irresistible. After nibbling on her neck the way she likes, I pulled her panties down and slipped inside her. I made love to her slowly for a while, cradling her against me. She was nervous about being loud, but I'm pretty sure my brothers weren't paying any attention to our tent. She was sexy as hell, coming with her hand clamped over her mouth, her eyes rolling back in her head.

The thought of it gets me hard again.

She wakes up just as I start to hear movement in the campsite. Someone is building a fire and low voices carry through our tent wall. Getting dressed is a little awkward. My tent is small, with a low ceiling, but we make it work. We come out and enjoy coffee and scrambled eggs, cooked over the fire.

I finish off the last of my coffee and take a quick lap around the campsite, testing my leg. It hurt like hell yesterday, probably from the drive. But it loosened up overnight and today it's back to normal.

"What do you think, Ems?" I ask. "Should we go for a hike?"

"Only if you promise not to get us lost this time," she says.

Ryan laughs and opens his mouth like he's going to give me shit, but I cut him off.

"Shut your face, Ryan."

"Hey, man, I didn't say a word," he says. "I just hope they taught you how to follow a map."

I laugh and shake my head. "Okay, photo boy."

He shrugs and points to Nicole. "I have a hot wife. Your taunts are meaningless."

"You guys want to join us?" I ask.

"Actually, Nic and I are going to run into town and get marshmallows and chocolate," Ryan says. "She wants s'mores tonight."

I glance over at Cody's tent. He and Clover haven't shown their faces yet, and there's no way I'm knocking on their tent door to see if they want to come hiking.

"Guess it's just you and me," I tell Emma.

I grab water and a few snacks and toss them into a backpack, then Emma and I head for the trail. There are several trailheads right in the campground, and after consulting a big map, we pick one and head out. There's a waterfall at the end, and if I remember correctly, we'll be able to climb down some rocks and get behind it.

"Do you remember that trail we hiked just outside of town?" she asks as we walk. "That summer before senior year?"

"With the blackberries?" I ask. "Unfortunately, yes, I do."

Emma laughs. "You just had to try to reach those berries at the top. You got so scratched up."

"You have a wonderful memory for our hiking disasters."

"It seems like there were a lot of them," she says.

"I guess we'll just have to start making new memories," I say. "Better ones."

Emma doesn't answer and we keep walking up the trail. We come to a steeper climb, and I have to slow down or I risk aggravating my knee. It feels good to move and get my blood pumping. Ever since I had to lie around for weeks in a hospital bed, I get anxious when I have to spend too much time sitting.

The sounds of the forest surround us, but we don't see any sign of other people. Tall fir trees tower over our heads, filtering the sunlight, and thick green underbrush spreads out alongside the trail. The roar of a waterfall grows in the distance.

We come to a spot where the trail levels off, then dips down again. The noise of water gets louder, and we round a corner, past a rock face jutting up on one side. Water cascades down a cliff, rushing toward the ground in a spray of white.

"I think the trail goes behind the water," I say. "Want to go down there and see?"

"Will we get wet?" she asks.

I like hearing her say *wet*. "Maybe a little."

I lead the way down the trail. A fine mist hangs in the air

as we get close, and the roar grows louder. It looks like the trail ends at the waterfall, but it continues on behind the sheet of water. Everything glistens from the spray and the hard-packed trail is muddy beneath our feet.

We duck through and the sound of the water fills the cave.

"This is amazing," Emma says. She walks forward and brushes her hand through the waterfall. It sprays back at her, the water bouncing off her hand.

"It's beautiful, isn't it?" I ask. I step forward and use my sleeve to wipe the water from her chin.

"Yeah, this is really great," she says.

I lean down and brush my lips against hers. She smells faintly of campfire, which is strangely arousing. I slide my hand around to the back of her neck and kiss her harder. She clutches my arms, parting her lips for my tongue. I love being able to kiss her whenever I want. After all the time I spent holding back, I can't seem to get enough of her.

"I don't know how you make me feel this way," she says.

I brush the hair back from her face. "What way?"

"Like I want you all the time," she says. Fuck, I love hearing her say that. "And like I can do anything with you. I can be myself. A version of myself I wasn't sure existed anymore."

"Of course you can," I say. "I think you're amazing."

Her lips turn up in a smile and there's a glint in her eye. "I feel like I can be a little naughty with you."

I like where this is going. I pull her closer. "Yeah? Naughty sounds fun."

She bites her lip and her eyes dart around. Her hand moves down to my groin and she strokes me through my jeans.

"Oh, Ems, you better not do that," I say.

"Are you sure?" she asks, a little hint of wickedness in her tone as she starts unfastening my pants.

I look around. We haven't seen anyone else on the trail, but that doesn't mean we won't. I back up until I hit the cave wall and Emma frees my erection from my pants. She licks her lips and lowers herself down.

*Oh, shit.*

She takes my cock in her mouth, keeping one hand on the shaft. Part of me wonders if I should be worried about someone coming down the trail, but that thought gets a lot less important as the feel of her mouth on my dick floods through me.

My cock slides against her tongue, and holy fuck it feels good. It isn't just that she has me in her mouth. It's that she's doing it out here, in the open. There's a hint of danger that turns me on like crazy. I put my hands through her hair, keeping my grip gentle, and watch. Her head moves back and forth, and she pulls out a little, sucking on the tip.

"Fuck, Emma, that feels so good."

She lifts her eyes and looks at me—looks right at me while she sucks my cock—and holy shit, it's the hottest thing I've ever seen in my life.

I enjoy the feel of her mouth on my cock for a few more minutes, thrusting my hips into her. As much as I love it, I want to be inside her.

"Come here," I say, putting my fingers under her chin.

She sucks me hard one last time and gets up, licking her lips like I'm the best thing she's ever tasted. I grab her by the back of the neck and kiss her, then reach down to unzip her jeans. I plunge my hand down her pants, curling my fingers between her legs. She's dripping wet.

I yank her pants down below her ass and spin her around so she's facing the cave wall. She arches her back and I plunge into her wet pussy. She moans, and I reach around to rub her clit while I fuck her from behind.

"Hurry before someone comes," she says.

"You're going to come," I say into her ear. "Come for me, baby."

I keep rubbing her clit, feeling her heat build. Her orgasm comes out of nowhere, and suddenly she's crying out, loud, as if there couldn't be anyone around to hear her. The sound of her voice and the feel of her pussy pulsing around me sends me over the edge, and I unload into her. I thrust hard, holding tight to her hips, coming with fury.

I slow down, sliding in and out a few more times as my orgasm ends. She looks at me over her shoulder and blinks a few times, like she forgot where she was.

She straightens and pulls up her pants. "Oh god, did we just do that?"

I'm pretty sex-drunk, and it takes me a second to realize I should probably put my dick away. I smile at her as I zip my pants, and she laughs.

I gather her up in my arms and run my fingers through her hair. "You are so fucking sexy."

"I can't believe I did that."

I kiss her mouth, deep and slow. "I can't believe it either. Are you all right?"

She nods, keeping her arms around my neck, her face close to mine. "Yes. I'm wonderful."

"Me too, Ems."

*Me too.*

## 19

# EMMA

*A*shlyn and I wander down the street with lattes in hand. The fall air has a bite to it; the breeze coming off the ocean is colder than it was just a few weeks ago. It's Saturday, so we're both off work. We had lunch and decided to do some window shopping down Main Street.

"So, anything new happening with your man?" I ask.

Ashlyn shrugs. Her hair has streaks of blue instead of pink, and she's wearing jeans and a gray sweater with a big yellow daisy on the front. "Not really. He's been fun, but I don't think it's going anywhere. What about you? How are things with Hunter?"

"Well," I say, pausing. "I went camping with him and his brothers a few weeks ago. We had a good time."

"Hanging out with the family?" Ashlyn asks. "That's getting serious."

"No," I say. "It's not getting serious. I used to love camping and I haven't been in years, so I decided to go."

"Okay," she says, and I don't miss the hint of sarcasm.

"What?"

"So, you guys are still just friends," she says. "And, maybe, kind of fucking on the side."

"Um, sort of?"

"You're so funny," Ashlyn says. "Why don't you just admit you're dating."

"I do admit we're dating. Kind of dating," I say. "But that doesn't mean it's serious. I'm not ready for that."

Ashlyn laughs.

"Why are you laughing at me?"

"I know casual flings," she says. "God knows I've had 'em. And you don't go camping with his family when you're just screwing around."

"I said we're kind of dating," I say.

"So what's stopping you from being *actually* dating, instead of *kind of* dating?" she asks.

We wander a little farther down the street and sit down on a bench.

"Honestly?" I say. "A lot of things. He's Hunter, for one. We have such a bleak history."

"True," she says. "Although, I'd hate for someone to judge me now based on the stupid stuff I did when I was eighteen."

I look down at my coffee. She does have a point. "Sure, but I wasn't kidding when I said I swore off men. I need time to figure out who I am again, and whether a man even fits into my future."

"I can see that."

"Plus ... I don't know if he's being totally open with me," I say.

"How so?"

"It's just a feeling," I say. "Sometimes I wonder if there's something going on and he's keeping it from me on purpose."

"Or maybe you're looking for something to be wrong," Ashlyn says. "Because things are starting to go right."

I don't really have an answer for that, so I take a sip of coffee. My cup is almost empty.

"Okay, but you have to tell me one thing," Ashlyn says. "You went camping with his brothers. Is Cody Jacobsen still super-hot? I had such a crush on him back in the day. Do you remember that?"

I laugh. "I remember. Super-hot or not, he's super-engaged now."

"Damn," she says. "Oh well."

I smile at her. It's so good to have a friend again.

AFTER SAYING GOODBYE TO ASHLYN, I head to my car. I haven't heard from Hunter today, and we don't have plans to hang out, but I really want to see him. I debate sending him a text to see if he's free, but decide to swing by his house and surprise him instead. I think he'll enjoy having me drop by unannounced. I've been the one holding back, and maybe it's time I let him in a little more.

His house isn't far from downtown. I stop at the stop sign just before his place and hesitate. There's a car I don't recognize parked on the street in front of his house. I take a deep breath, telling myself to stop being so paranoid. There are a million reasons someone could have parked there. It doesn't mean something bad.

An older woman gets out of the driver's side. She's dressed in dark pants and a light coat, her gray hair pulled up. My shoulders relax.

*God, Emma, what were you so worried about? That a hot blonde was going to get out of the car?*

I hesitate at the corner. I'm not sure who the woman is, and I don't want to intrude. I should definitely drive away.

Hunter walks out his front door. I see him approach the car, a big smile on his face. The back car door opens, and he crouches down. A little boy, maybe five or six years old, jumps out of the car and leaps into his arms.

My heart stops. *Oh my god.*

Could that be...? Does Hunter have a son?

Hunter stands, the little boy's arms wrapped around his neck. He reaches into the car and brings out a bright blue backpack, then carries the boy toward his front door. The woman follows them inside.

My hands shake as I drive away. Is this what he's been hiding from me? I think about all the phone calls he's taken in private, walking away so I don't hear what he's saying. All the times he's said he's busy, but hasn't told me what he's doing. I tried to tell myself it must be his job—he doesn't work normal hours, and I know a lot of what he does is confidential. But that explanation never felt right. If he was taking work calls, or running training sessions at his property, wouldn't he just tell me? Why avoid it altogether?

Because it wasn't about work.

My instincts have been screaming at me. I should have listened. I knew there was something he was keeping from me, but I never would have guessed he has a child.

Why would he hide it? Why not just tell me?

I wonder who the mother is, and why someone else was dropping the kid off with Hunter. Is the woman I saw the boy's grandmother? Why would she bring the boy to see Hunter? I suppose the mother could be working. Or Hunter and the boy's mother have a contentious relationship, so the grandmother has to be the go-between.

That's a disturbing thought.

I get home and pour myself a glass of wine. I have no idea what to do now. I don't want him to think I was spying on him. But I can't pretend I didn't see.

## 20

## HUNTER

*I*saac didn't want me to drop him off at Elaine's after his overnight stay. I drive away from her house, my heart in my throat, my shoulder still damp from his tears. I think Elaine was worried I kept him up too late when he stayed at my place, and he fell apart because he was overtired. But he slept great at my house. I wore him out pretty good, and he fell asleep minutes after I tucked him in. He even slept until after eight this morning. When I told him he had to go home today, he frowned, and his big eyes filled with tears. I wound up staying at Elaine's until his bedtime, and he still cried when I had to leave.

He broke my fucking heart. I didn't want him to go home either.

I've been thinking a lot about Isaac, and Elaine. I'm pretty sure I know what I need to do—what I want to do—but it's such a big change. I don't know if I'm ready. Having him for a couple of days is one thing. But what I'm contemplating is a lot more than that. The thought scares the crap out of me.

I need to talk to Emma. I still haven't told her about

Isaac. She and I still feel so damn fragile. She's come a long way—from declaring herself on a relationship moratorium, to definitely being in a relationship with me. We're in full-on phase three, and the only thing keeping us out of phase four is that I haven't heard her refer to me as her boyfriend yet. But when I tell her about Isaac—which is a complicated situation to begin with—is that going to scare her off?

She's keeping me at a careful distance, and I respect that. I resolved from the beginning that I'd give her the time and space she needs to learn to trust me again. I need to ease her into the idea that Isaac is a part of my life. That's a pretty big bombshell to drop on someone, especially because, eventually, I plan to be taking Isaac to Elaine's house for visits, not the other way around.

A week later, I'm starting to worry that Emma is purposefully avoiding me. She doesn't answer my texts right away, if at all, which is unusual. I call her to see if she wants to get together, and she says she's too busy with work.

But there's something in her voice that raises a big red flag. It's not just her use of the words, "I'm fine," although that should be enough to get any man ready for combat. I can tell she's not telling me something, and the fact that she avoids getting together puts me on the defensive.

By Friday night, I'm itching to see her. I've been busy all week with a training seminar at my property. They're a hard-working group, but it's for a private security firm, and they tend to be high maintenance. We finished early enough that they headed out of town this afternoon, so I decide to swing by Emma's. She said she was too busy to hang out tonight, but there's no way I can wait any longer.

I'm buzzing with adrenaline as I walk up to her door. I hate feeling like this. I glance over my shoulder several times, even though I know there isn't anyone watching me. Her reluctance to see me this week has me on edge.

I knock, and a few seconds later she answers. Her eyes widen when she sees me.

"Hi," she says.

"Hey," I say. She doesn't invite me in. "Um, sorry to drop by without calling. I was out, and I haven't seen you in a while. I missed you."

Her face softens a little and she steps aside. "Yeah, sorry, it's been a weird week."

She lets me in, but her body language is all wrong. Not only is there absolutely no affectionate greeting—no touching, no hug, no kiss—she's stiff and she won't look me in the eye.

The mission has definitely been compromised. I need to know why.

"So, have you been busy with work?" I ask, trying to sound casual. I take a seat at the dining table, where I have a good view of both the kitchen and living room. I don't want her to be able to disappear into another room.

"Yeah, so busy," she says. "I've had all these crazy deadlines. Sometimes they just don't understand I can only do so much."

She's lying.

I can see the lie. More than once, my life depended on my ability to judge whether someone was telling the truth. I got pretty good at reading people. Emma shook her head slightly when she said *yeah*. She doesn't believe her own words.

"Well, I hope you got caught up," I say.

"I did," she says. She hesitates near the table, her eyes darting to the kitchen, like she's not sure if she should sit down and talk to me or try to get away.

"I had a rough week, too," I say, trying to keep the conversation going. "Sometimes these guys think I'm supposed to be available twenty-four seven."

"Do you, um, want some water or something?" she asks.

Fuck, why is she acting like it's awkward having me here? I search my memory of the last time we were together. Did I do something to make her uncomfortable? I fucked her on my kitchen table, but it was her idea. I came out of the bathroom and she was sitting there, naked. She can't be mad about that, can she?

"I'm good," I say. She's not giving me anything, so I figure I just need to ask. "Ems, is something wrong?"

She walks into the kitchen and gets herself a glass of water. My back and shoulders tense up. She's not telling me something, and I'm starting to worry it might be a big deal. I feel like I'm walking point, leading a strike, about to duck around a corner and discover my intel was bad and I'm not prepared for what's coming.

"No, it's nothing," she says. Lying again.

"Are you sure?" I ask. "Because if there is something, maybe we should just talk about it."

"No, I'm fine," she says. She is *not* fine. "Gabe's working, as usual, so I was just going to watch a movie tonight. Do you want to watch something?"

"Sure," I say.

I get up and join her in the living room. I feel like explosives are planted all over the floor and if I step wrong, I'm going to get my shit blown up.

I sit down on the couch next to her, but she keeps a cushion length of distance between us.

"So," I say, hesitating. I want to ask her what the fuck is going on, but I'm afraid she'll just kick me out without telling me. "Did you have a movie in mind?"

"When were you going to tell me?" she asks, her voice quiet.

Shit, what does she mean? Is she talking about when I left her? I still haven't really explained myself—but fuck, it's hard to explain. "Tell you what?"

"That you have a kid, Hunter."

My mouth drops open and, for a second, I don't know what to say. "Wait, how do you know about Isaac?"

"Oh my god." Emma gets up and walks into the kitchen.

I stand up and hold out a hand. "No, wait. Slow down, Ems, because whatever you heard, you have the wrong idea."

"How could you keep something like this from me?" she asks.

"Let me explain—"

"Explain what? That you've been lying to me about your son?"

"He's not my son."

Emma stops and meets my eyes. "What?"

"He's not my son," I say. "I don't have a child."

Her eyebrows draw together in confusion. "Then who is Isaac?"

"His father was Major Anthony Lynch," I say. "I served with him. Anthony's girlfriend Mary died when Isaac was born, and Anthony's mother took care of Isaac when Anthony was deployed." I pause, taking a deep breath. "Anthony didn't come home from his last deployment. Before he died, I promised him if something ever happened, I'd look after his son."

Emma puts a hand to her mouth and stares at me.

I rub the back of my neck. "I see Isaac about once a week, if I can. Sometimes I take him overnight. His grandma, Elaine, has a lot of health problems, so I do what I can to help them out. I probably should have told you about him before now. I just wasn't sure what to say."

"Why? Why didn't you just tell me?"

"I wanted to, but I know you're not ready for anything serious," I say. "Even though he's not mine, he's a big part of my life. Sharing that with you felt like a big deal."

"Oh god, Hunter, I..." She trails off, looking away. "I'm so sorry. I drove by your house and saw you get him out of the car. I assumed he was yours, and you didn't want me to know for some reason."

I walk into the kitchen and slip my hands around Emma's waist. "It was stupid of me not to tell you. I was just ... worried that it would freak you out."

She leans her head on my chest. "You're such a good man."

I smile and kiss the top of her head. "Tell you what ... do you want to meet him?"

She looks up at me. "Really?"

"Of course," I say. "I wasn't sure if I was going to make it out there tomorrow, but we can at least take him to get ice cream or something."

She hesitates, looking away, and I can tell she's thinking it over. Finally, she looks up at me. "Sure, I'd love to."

We pull up in front of Elaine's house Saturday afternoon, and Isaac is out the door before I can turn off the truck. I jump out and circle around so he won't run into the road, and scoop him up in my arms.

"Hey, buddy." I ruffle his hair. "How's my favorite kindergartner?"

"Good," he says. "But I got in trouble by my teacher."

"Uh oh," I say. "What happened?"

His lower lip sticks out a little and he looks down. "I threw some crayons."

"Why did you do that?"

"I was mad."

"Aw, buddy." My throat tightens. If anyone understands what it's like to be a mad kid, it's me. "Did you apologize?"

"Yes."

"That's good," I say. "You know, it's okay to feel mad. We all feel mad or angry once in a while. But it's not okay to throw things."

"I know," he says. "I had to stay inside at recess."

"Yeah, well, sometimes we have to take our punishment, right?" I say. "Were you a big man about it?"

"Yes," he says. "I helped my teacher instead of playing."

"You're a good boy, Isaac," I say. "I'm proud of you."

Emma steps out of the truck and Isaac's eyes widen. "Who is that?"

"This is my friend, Emma," I say. I *almost* introduce her as my girlfriend, but I stop myself at the last second. She needs to be the first one to say it.

"Hi, Isaac," Emma says.

Isaac buries his face in my shoulder.

"It's okay, buddy, you can talk to her," I say. "I know she's really pretty. She makes me feel shy, too."

Emma laughs, but Isaac doesn't look up.

"I have an idea," I say. "I think Emma might like some ice cream. Do you think we should take her to get some?"

Isaac pops up with a smile. "Can I come, too?"

"Yeah," I say. "That's a great idea. Let's get your shoes on and ask your grandma if it's okay."

We take Isaac out for ice cream. He sits between Emma and me in the booth—he insists he wants to sit next to both of us, so we squeeze in on one side. He licks his scoop of chocolate, getting it on his chin. It starts to melt, running down his arm. We go through a lot of napkins trying to keep him clean.

Isaac warms up to Emma so quickly, I'm amazed. He's usually very shy around people he doesn't know, but he tells her all about his new school and his favorite cartoons. He looks like he might cry when we drop him off, but he glances up at Emma and holds back his tears. I give him a big hug and kiss the top of his head, promising I'll see him again in a week. He holds his arms out to Emma, wanting a hug, and it's all I can do not to get choked up.

After we say our goodbyes, I drive us back to Jetty Beach, the sun setting as we head down the highway.

"Isaac is a great kid," Emma says.

I smile. "He really is. He's amazing."

"Can I tell you something?" she asks.

I glance at her and she looks at me shyly. "Sure."

"Seeing you with him was really sexy," she says. "I don't want to go home. Can I stay at your place tonight?"

I grin at her. "Baby, the answer to that is always yes."

*I* feel like I owe Hunter a bigger apology than I can give with words. As soon as we're back at his place, I rip off his pants and give him the best fucking blowjob I know how to give. I wasn't kidding when I said seeing him with Isaac was sexy. There's something about that man, with those big strong arms, turning to putty for a little five-year-old kid. I melted a little when I saw them together.

Okay, I melted a *lot*.

I was relieved to find out Hunter wasn't hiding a child from me, and I can understand why he didn't tell me about Isaac. I've been the one keeping my distance, being hesitant with Hunter. I feel like I'm justified, but I also can't blame him for being unsure of how much to share with me. We're taking this slow, as we should be.

We have a late dinner and curl up on the couch together to watch TV for a while. I doze off with my head in his lap. I don't know what time it is when he carries me to bed. He sets me down gently and gets in bed with me, and I relax against his warm body, comfortable and content.

A noise wakes me from a dead sleep. My eyes fly open; my heart races. I pull the sheet up over my chest and look around the dark room, blinking hard. Was I dreaming? Did I really hear something? I glance over to see if whatever it was woke Hunter.

He's not there.

I'm still half asleep and my brain struggles to catch up. A sliver of soft light leaks in through a crack in the curtains, and I see Hunter sitting on the edge of the bed. He's leaning down with his head in his hands.

"Hunter?"

He doesn't answer.

I sit up and scoot across the bed, getting closer to him. He's breathing hard, his shoulders and back flexing with every breath. I lift a hand to caress his skin, but I'm suddenly afraid to touch him. He's so tense.

"Hunter, are you all right?" I ask, my voice quiet.

"No," he says, clutching his chest. "Can't breathe."

My hands tremble, but something tells me I need to be the one to stay calm. I carefully place a hand on his shoulder. He flinches, but I get closer, running my hand along his back.

"You're okay," I say.

He shakes his head, buries it in his hands again. "Fuck. I can't."

He starts to stand up, but I grab his arm and gently hold onto his wrist. I might be doing the wrong thing, but I don't want him to walk away from me. He sits down, but his entire body is wound up tight. This is what he was talking about—losing control. Panicking. I've never seen him like this, and fear rolls through me, but I desperately want to help.

I get on my knees so I can press myself closer to him and

put an arm around his shoulders. I lean in to speak softly into his ear.

"Hunter, listen to me. You're okay." I rub my hand across his bare back. He's breathing too fast, his body shaking. "I'm here. You're okay. Baby, you're safe."

He looks at me, his forehead furrowed, a deep groove between his eyebrows. I put my hand to his cheek and touch my forehead to his.

"You're safe," I whisper.

He pulls me into his lap and I wrap my legs around his waist. He puts his arms around me, holding me close, and buries his face in my neck. I run my hands through his hair and across his shoulders. His thick arms are so strong. I whisper into his ear, hoping my words will reassure him. His breathing slows to a more normal pace and his grip on me loosens.

"I'm sorry," he says into my neck, his voice muffled.

I hold him tighter. "Don't be sorry. Were you dreaming?"

"I think so."

I stroke the back of his neck. "You're okay, now. You're here with me."

His arms tighten around me again. I feel his lips on my skin, kissing my shoulder. He moves up my neck and I lean my head to the side. His cock hardens against me and I tilt my hips, rubbing against him through my panties.

He makes a low noise in his throat and grabs my hips, his grip firm. He twists, flipping me onto my back. His mouth takes mine, his tongue hard and aggressive. He pushes my panties to the side and pulls out his cock. He rams into me, hard, but I'm already so wet he slips in easily.

He pulls back to look at me, his eyes steely. His face is so intense. He holds himself up with one hand, his other grabbing my hip, and thrusts himself in, over and over, fucking me with fury. I lose myself in his onslaught, digging my fingers into his back, calling out with every thrust.

My head spins; the whole world falls away. I open my legs so he can go deeper, so he can sink every bit of himself into me. I want him to feel nothing but my pussy. I want to fuck the fear and pain right out of him.

He leans down, kissing my neck, growling. I feel his tight control slipping, and I want him to keep going. I want him to unleash.

I want him to know he can.

Without warning, he stops, his cock buried in my pussy. He breathes hard against my neck. His back is slick with sweat.

"Don't stop," I say.

He takes a few more breaths. I rock back and forth, squeezing him as hard as I can. God, he feels so good. His hand grips my ass and he groans. "I need to be careful with you," he says.

"No you don't," I say. "Give it all to me, Hunter. I want it."

He pulls out and manhandles me onto my knees, then drives his cock in deep from behind, holding tight to my hips.

"Yes, harder," I say, my voice nothing more than a whimper.

He fucks me like a storm breaking, his thrusts hard and intense. I used to hate being on my knees, but with Hunter it feels good—a dirty kind of good that I want to let out. I want to be this woman with him, uninhibited and raw.

"Oh, god, Hunter, fuck me harder."

I reach down to rub my clit while he pounds me. I've never touched myself like this in front of someone, but I do it without hesitation. It makes my pussy heat up fast, wet and burning around his cock.

"Fuck, Emma."

He pulls out and turns me onto my back again. He pushes my legs up so my knees are to my shoulders, and slides his cock back in. This new angle is divine; his body grinds against my clit with every thrust. I feel so vulnerable, so open. So alive.

Hunter's cock throbs inside me. He goes in so deep, bottoming out, filling me completely. My head swims as my climax builds. He takes me to the edge, fucking me madly, unleashing his aggression.

Then I lose control, spinning with lust, calling his name into the night. His body stiffens and he groans, spilling himself into me. I think I'm finished, but his orgasm heats me up again, and my pussy clenches, throbs, tightens. The pulses come from deep inside, my core muscles contracting around him over and over.

When we both finish, he stops and pulls out, gently lowering my legs to the bed. He blinks at me hard, like he's waking from a dream. His chest moves fast with his breathing, his rippling abs tight.

"Fuck, Emma," he says. He lies down next to me and scoops me into his arms, kissing me gently. He leans his forehead against mine. "Are you okay?"

"That was amazing," I say. I can still feel him inside me, and I know it will be a while before that feeling goes away.

He's silent for a long moment, staring at me as he caresses my cheek. "Thank you for helping me calm down."

"I'm glad I could," I say. "What happened?"

"I don't know," he says. "It was probably a dream, but I don't remember. I woke up feeling like there was a weight on my chest. I couldn't get enough air."

I tilt my face closer and brush a kiss against his lips.

"I don't like being out of control," he says.

"If that's what you do to me when you're out of control, don't fight it so hard," I say.

"I'm afraid to push you too far."

I snuggle into his arms and he pulls me against him. "Don't be."

Sleepiness overtakes me and I relax into his warmth. He holds me tight, and I feel the soft rhythm of his breathing as I go to sleep in his arms.

—————

## 22

## EMMA

*I* drive over to Hunter's house after I finish work. He's been working hard all week, so we have plans for a low key evening—dinner and a movie. I know he's pretty worn out, but I think I'll be able to convince him to have some dessert after we get back to his place—and I don't mean cake.

Hunter answers the door, pulling me in for a kiss. I relax against him, parting my lips for his tongue. His hands hold my waist, his kiss deep. I love the way he kisses me. He takes my breath away.

"Wow," I breathe when he pulls away. I feel a little dizzy.

He rubs his nose against mine. "It's good to see you, Ems."

"You too."

He gives me another quick kiss, then drops his hands. "What sounds good? I'm starving."

I notice he's limping more than usual as he walks to get his keys off the kitchen counter.

"I'm good with whatever," I say. "Are you okay?"

He winces. "Yeah. I overdid it and I'm paying for it today.

But I don't have any sessions scheduled for the next week, so I'll be fine."

When he comes close, I rub my hand along his hip and around to his ass. "Maybe I can make you feel better later."

He smiles. "I'm sure you can."

We go outside and get in his truck.

"Something simple like burgers sounds good," he says as he pulls out of his driveway. "What do you think?"

I smile at him. "Great."

His phone rings and his eyebrows draw in as he looks at the screen. "I don't recognize this number, but I'll just take it real quick."

"Sure."

"Hello." Hunter listens for a moment, his expression darkening. "Yes, I'm Hunter Evans. Yes. I do. What hospital? No, no, do not do that. No, I'll be there. Please, don't do that. Keep him there, I'm on my way right now."

He hangs up and his face is tense. "Elaine was just rushed to the hospital and they're going to put Isaac in a foster home if I don't pick him up."

"Oh, no," I say, my breath catching.

Hunter turns, taking us toward the highway.

It's a forty-five minute drive to the hospital. Hunter is silent the entire trip, gripping the steering wheel, veins standing out on his forearms beneath his tattoos. I wish I could say something to make him feel better, but I know there's nothing I can do.

We park outside the emergency room and go inside. Hunter hurries to the desk.

"I'm Hunter Evans," he says. "Elaine Lynch was brought in earlier. I'm here to pick up her grandson, Isaac."

The man at the desk nods and picks up his phone.

Hunter opens and closes his fists. I can see the tension in his back and shoulders.

We wait in the lobby for about five minutes before someone comes to bring us back. Hunter's back is stiff and straight, and his limp fades to almost nothing as he strides down the hall. I have to hurry to keep up.

The nurse leads us to another waiting room. Isaac is there, sitting in a chair, hugging his knees to his chest. A middle-aged woman in a button-down shirt and slacks is sitting next to him.

"Uncle Hunter!" Isaac jumps out of his chair and runs toward us. Hunter crouches down to one knee and scoops Isaac up in his arms. The woman approaches, and I hesitate next to Hunter. I suddenly feel out of place, like I shouldn't be here.

Isaac looks so small in Hunter's big arms.

"Hi, buddy," Hunter says. "Are you okay?"

Isaac nods, not letting go of Hunter's neck.

"I'm sorry you had to wait for me," Hunter says.

"Mr. Evans?" the woman says.

Hunter stands, picking up Isaac effortlessly and shifting him to one arm. "Yes."

"I'm Erin Strauss with Social Services," she says. She hands Hunter Isaac's blue backpack. "Thanks for coming."

"Of course," Hunter says. He puts the backpack at his feet and shakes hands with her.

"I'm sorry we didn't call you sooner," Erin says. "There was some confusion as to what was to be done with Isaac in case of an emergency."

"How long has he been here?" Hunter asks. He rubs his hand across Isaac's back.

"A few hours," she says.

Hunter's eyes widen. "Hours?" He clamps his mouth shut, as if he's biting back his words.

"I'll need to see some I.D. before I can let you take Isaac," she says.

"Sure." He pulls his wallet out of his back pocket and opens it for her. Isaac keeps his face buried in Hunter's neck. "Where's Elaine?"

"She's in ICU," Erin says. "But she's conscious. She'd like to see you before you go, but children aren't allowed."

"Okay." He turns to me. "Could you wait with him while I go talk to Elaine?"

"Yeah, of course," I say.

"I'll let them know you're coming," Erin says. "Someone will bring you back to see her." She walks away.

"Hey, big guy," Hunter says, and rubs Isaac's back again. "I need to go talk to your grandma for a few minutes, but I'm going to come right back. Then I'm going to take you home to my house. Do you want to come stay with me?"

Isaac nods, but doesn't lift his face.

"Good. Okay, so while I go see your grandma, Emma is going to hang out with you here. You remember Emma, right? We all had ice cream together."

Isaac doesn't move.

"Bud, I know you don't want me to put you down, but I promise I won't leave you," Hunter says, his voice soft. "You can trust me."

Tears sting my eyes, and I swallow hard.

"Isaac," I say. Hunter nods and I put my hand on Isaac's back. "Hey sweetie, can I hold you for a few minutes?"

Isaac nods again. Without quite lifting his face, he peels away from Hunter and reaches for me.

My heart breaks into a million pieces. I take him from Hunter and balance him on my hip, my arms around him.

He threads his little arms around my neck and puts his face down on my shoulder.

Hunter rubs his back. "I'll be right back, buddy."

A nurse in blue scrubs is waiting nearby and Hunter follows him out, through a set of wide double doors.

I lower myself down onto a chair and shrug my purse off my shoulder onto the seat next to me. Isaac settles into my lap, still keeping a death grip on my neck. I sit with him for a while, rubbing slow circles across his back, rocking back and forth in my seat. Slowly, his body relaxes.

"You've had a hard day, haven't you?" I say.

Isaac nods.

"Sounds like you had to wait here a long time. Were you scared?"

He nods again and I squeeze him tighter.

"I'm sorry that was scary," I say. "Uncle Hunter didn't know what happened. He came as fast as he could."

"Is Grandma okay?" he asks in a tiny voice.

"I don't know, sweetie," I say. "But the doctors are taking such good care of her."

He trembles and I hug him again. He feels so small and fragile in my arms. I can't imagine everything he's been through: losing his parents, being raised by his grandmother. I desperately hope Elaine will get better. I don't know if he has any other family. This poor, sweet boy has already lost so much. It's so damn unfair.

I close my eyes, rocking him slowly, keeping my arms around him. He's so tiny and innocent, with skinny arms and knobby knees. I want to shield him from all the fear and pain in the world.

We wait a while before Hunter returns. I can't see a clock, and I don't want to let go of Isaac to check my phone, but it must be at least half an hour. He doesn't move his head from my shoulder, but his arms eventually drop to his sides and his back moves up and down in a slow rhythm. I'm pretty sure he's sleeping.

Hunter walks into the waiting room and pauses, looking at us. I give him a little smile.

"Is he asleep?" Hunter asks, his voice quiet.

"I think so," I whisper. "How's Elaine?"

Hunter shakes his head. "Not good. She's going to be here a while. We should get home."

I nod. Hunter carefully takes Isaac, who stirs and rubs his eyes.

"It's time to go," Hunter says.

"Am I going to your house?" Isaac asks.

"Yeah, buddy."

I grab the backpack, and we take Isaac to Hunter's truck. He gets Isaac strapped into his booster seat, then we both get in the front and ride back to Jetty Beach in silence.

## 23 - Hunter

ISAAC IS STILL awake when we pull up to my house. I get him out of the truck while Emma takes his backpack inside. His little arms curl around my neck again as I carry him in.

I'm still trying to stay in control of the flash of anger I felt when the social worker told me Isaac had been at the hospital for hours. They should have called me, immediately. Elaine had instructions on file with the hospital. Someone should have known. My poor little man must have been terrified. I hope no one said the words "foster home" in his hearing. I'm not sure if he knows what that means, but I don't ever want him to think that's an option.

I put Isaac down on the couch. "I'll get you something to eat, okay, buddy?"

He scoots into the corner, tucking his feet beneath him. I give Emma a reassuring smile, and she sits down next to him.

I go into the kitchen in search of something to feed him. I don't have much, but he isn't picky. I pull out some bread and peanut butter.

"Do you like honey or jelly on your sandwich, bud?" I ask.

"Honey," Isaac says.

I hear a zipper and glance into the living room. Isaac pulls his Spiderman action figure out of his backpack. I'm glad someone thought to pack something for him. I wonder if it was the paramedics or if a social worker went to his house. I'm still not clear on how he ended up at the hospital.

"Is that your favorite toy?" Emma asks.

"Yeah."

I move so I have a view of the couch while I make his sandwich.

"What do you like about him?" she asks.

"Well," Isaac says, turning his action figure over in his hand and scrutinizing it. "He's a superhero and he saves people. And he shoots webs."

"That is so cool," Emma says.

I grab the honey out of the cupboard, glad I still have some.

"And he's like me," Isaac says.

"How is he like you?" she asks.

"His parents died, too."

My throat closes up. Oh god.

"That's very sad," Emma says, her voice soft.

"Yeah," Isaac says.

"You're lucky to have someone like your Uncle Hunter to help take care of you," she says.

"Uncle Hunter is a superhero, too," Isaac says, his voice brightening.

"He is?" Emma says. "How is he a superhero?"

"He's big and strong," Isaac says. "And Grandma says he saved people, like Spiderman. But I don't think he shoots webs. I think he's more like Iron Man."

This kid is going to make me fucking cry.

I take a few deep breaths and swallow down the lump in my throat. *Just make the damn sandwich, Hunter. Don't lose your shit in front of these two.*

I cut the crusts off and toss them in the garbage, and put the sandwich on a plate. I'm just about to bring it out to Isaac when I hear his voice again.

"Are you Uncle Hunter's girlfriend?" he asks. "I know what that means. When you're boyfriend and girlfriend it means you like each other more than a friend and maybe you'll get married."

I freeze, my heart suddenly pounding.

"Um, yeah, I guess I am his girlfriend."

I let out a long breath. Phase four. Unfortunately, I think I'm about to sabotage the mission.

I wait another beat to make sure I have my shit together, and bring Isaac his sandwich. "Here you go, buddy," I say. "It's late, so eat this up and then it's bedtime, okay?"

He nods and takes a bite of his sandwich.

I meet Emma's eyes and nod toward the door. "Hey, can I talk to you out here for a second?"

She stands and picks up her purse.

"I'll be right back, bud," I say to Isaac.

Emma follows me outside and I gently shut the door behind her.

"Sorry our plans got derailed tonight," I say.

She shakes her head. "Don't be. Of course I don't mind. Isaac is so sweet."

I smile, despite the ache in my chest. "Yeah, he's amazing."

"Do you think Elaine is going to be okay?"

"Honestly, I don't know. She's been having health problems for a long time." I pause and take a deep breath. I don't want to do this. I know this is going to push her away. But I have to. It isn't just about me anymore. "Ems, you should probably head home tonight, instead of staying over."

"Oh," she says, and I can hear the hurt in her voice. "Okay."

"It's just..." How do I explain this to her? "Isaac has lost so much already. I can't let him get attached to you if I'm not sure that you're always going to be around."

"I don't know if I understand what you're saying," she says.

I take a deep breath. There's nothing I can do but be honest. "Emma, when it comes to this"—I gesture back and forth between the two of us—"I'm all in. I'm in this for the long haul, and I mean that. But I know you aren't there yet. I'm willing to be patient and give you as much time as you need. I can't stand the thought of losing you. But," I say, taking another breath, "I've already talked to Elaine about taking custody of Isaac, permanently. It's something I've been thinking about for a long time. Even if she gets better, Isaac is five. She can't do this for the next thirteen years. But I can. And if I'm going to do that, I'm going to make a commitment to him, and that commitment has to be forever. I want this, and I want you to be a part of it, but I know I can't ask that of you right now. I want to be what you need, but I have to be what Isaac needs, too. And he needs stability, and people in his life who are going to stay."

She opens her mouth, but doesn't say anything. I know it's too much. She's barely able to admit we're dating again. I feel so hollow inside, but I don't have a choice.

"I know this is huge," I continue. "It might seem like it's coming out of nowhere, but I knew this day was coming. You have to understand what Isaac has been through. He lost his mother when he was born. His dad died when he was so young he'll barely remember him. He has no one else. If someone doesn't step in and be a fucking man for this kid, he's going to turn out like me, only worse. I was redeemable. He won't be."

"Hunter, what are you saying?" she asks. "That we either get married, or break up?"

"No, that's not what I mean," I say. *But fuck, Emma, I'd marry you tomorrow.* "But what do you think will happen if you stay tonight, and the three of us have breakfast together tomorrow? And the next day? We play with him at the park, take him to school, tuck him into bed at night together? He's going to think we're a family. That this is his life now, and you're in it. What happens if that changes? What happens if you decide this isn't what you want? That *we* aren't what you want? If it was just me, I'd wait it out. I'd wait another ten years for you if that's what it took. But Isaac doesn't have that luxury. He needs people in his life who are going to stick. He'd be devastated to lose you. He's lost too many people already."

"Damn it, Hunter, what am I supposed to say?" she asks. "That I'm ready to jump in head first? I'm not."

I grind my teeth. I want to grab her and kiss her until she relents. I want to push her up against the door and overwhelm her so she can't say no. But I can't. I can't make her stay.

"Why are you so closed off to the possibility that this is real?" I ask, my voice laced with frustration. I'm trying to hold everything in, but my control is slipping.

"Gee, I wonder," she says. "I was convinced of it once, and look what happened."

I look away.

"You left me, Hunter." Her eyes glisten with tears. "You left me in the middle of the night, with no warning, no goodbye. For all I knew, you were dead."

"I know I made a mistake—"

"It was much more than a mistake," she says. "And you still won't tell me why."

I look down at the ground. I can't. She wants the truth, and I can't give it to her. She'll never look at me again if she knows.

"Still no?" she says. "I don't think you have any idea what you did to me when you left. It destroyed me. I was a wreck for so long, and I never really got over it. I've been carrying that around with me for a decade. And I hate it. I hate myself for being ruined by you. I can't let you do that to me again."

Before I can say another word, she storms off to her car.

*Fuck.*

I lean back against the door and watch her go. My heart starts to race, and my chest tightens. I need to calm down. I wait until her tail lights disappear, taking deep breaths to slow my heartbeat. I'd like to drown my frustration in whiskey tonight, but that's out of the question. I have a little boy to take care of now.

Inside, Isaac's plate is on the coffee table, nothing left

but crumbs. His backpack is on the couch next to him and he's playing with his action figures in his lap.

"Hey buddy," I say. "It's time for bed."

"Where's Emma?"

"She went home," I say.

"She doesn't live here with you?" he asks.

"No, bud, she doesn't," I say. "Emma's just a friend of mine."

His eyes are a little red and his lids droop low. He looks so tired. I take him to the bathroom and help him brush his teeth, then we find a pair of green camo pajamas in his backpack. He climbs into the extra bed, and I pull the covers up to his chin.

"Will you lie down with me?" he asks.

"Sure," I say. I get onto the bed next to him and lie on my side. He curls up against me, leaning his head on my arm. He smells like fresh cut grass and toothpaste.

"Uncle Hunter?" he says, his voice sleepy.

"Yeah, buddy?"

"I wish you were my dad."

I close my eyes against the flood of tears and swallow hard. I wrap him in my arms and hold him tight, kissing the top of his head. I'm too choked up to answer.

*Me too, buddy. Me too.*

## 23

## EMMA

*I* never should have come back to this stupid town. My clothes are strewn all over the bed, some folded, others in a loose pile. I emptied the closet, and my dresser, but the resulting mess is almost debilitating. My one suitcase is already full, and I didn't save any moving boxes.

I should have. This was only supposed to be temporary —a place to crash for a few weeks while I figure things out. Instead, I've been living with my brother for months, and sleeping with the man who crushed my soul when I was eighteen.

What the fuck was I thinking?

I need to get out of here. I have no idea where I'm going to go, but staying in this town is not an option.

My phone buzzes with a text and my heart nearly skips. Is it Hunter? But it's Ashlyn.

*Plans tonight? Wanna hang out?*

I hesitate, wondering what to say to her. *Sure. I could use some girl time. Life sucks.*

*Say no more. Be there shortly.*

There's a soft knock on the bedroom door, and Gabe peeks in through the crack. "What's going on in here? Reorganizing all your stuff?"

I keep folding. "I'm packing."

"Going somewhere?"

"I'm moving out."

He opens the door a little wider and leans against the frame. "Any particular reason?"

I stop, dropping a shirt onto the pile. "I shouldn't have come back here in the first place."

"What happened?" he asks. "Did Hunter..."

"No, he didn't disappear or anything," I say. "I don't know what I'm doing, Gabe. I was supposed to be putting my life back together. All I've done is make it worse."

I snatch the shirt back off the pile and start folding furiously again.

"Come on," Gabe says, putting a gentle hand on my shoulder. "Why don't you leave this for now. I'll open some wine."

I let out a heavy sigh. "Fine."

I follow him out to the living room and he gets us each a glass of Pinot Noir. He sits down on the other side of the couch. We sit in silence for a while, sipping our wine. I'm glad he doesn't ask questions right away. He deserves to know what's going on, but I feel so out of control.

A few minutes later, there's a knock at the front door.

"That's probably Ashlyn," I say.

"Are you in the mood for visitors?" Gabe asks.

"Yeah, it's fine," I say. "I invited her."

Gabe gets up to let her in. She's wearing an oversized t-shirt that drapes off one shoulder, and a pair of bright blue leggings.

"Wine?" Gabe asks.

"Definitely," she says, coming around to sit on the couch next to me. "What's up with the *life sucks* stuff? Is this about Hunter?"

Gabe hands her a glass and takes a seat in the chair next to us.

Where do I even begin? "I moved back here to get my shit together. I wanted to find who I am again, and figure out what I want out of my life. None of my plans have worked out the way I thought. I wanted to pick up the pieces and start over. But I feel like I'm right back where I was ten years ago."

"He didn't take off again, did he?" Ashlyn asks.

"No, he didn't," I say. "But why did I start seeing him again in the first place? It's Hunter. I don't know if I've ever been honest with either of you about how much he hurt me when he left. I literally got up one day, and he was gone. His family didn't know where he went. He left them a note, but he didn't say a word to me. His mom called me in a panic that morning. She thought maybe he and I ran off together. I'll never forget how terrified she sounded when I told her I didn't even know he was gone."

I take a sip of wine. Ashlyn and I were friends back then, but I've never shared the whole story with anyone.

"At first, we thought he might have committed suicide. His note didn't say what he'd done or where he'd gone. It just said he was sorry. What the fuck did that mean? We were literally searching for a body. I've never been so scared in my life. Eventually, someone contacted his parents and they found out he'd enlisted in the Marines. But it would still be months before they heard from him directly. Months. It was like he walked off the face of the Earth, as if none of us were still here to care what had become of him."

"Holy shit," Ashlyn says.

"I fell apart," I say. "Completely fell apart. I couldn't sleep. I barely ate anything. It was literally the worst thing I've ever been through. It was worse than when Dad left. Worse than my divorce. It messed me up for a long time. And looking back, I hate that about myself. I hate that I was such a weak little girl. I let some guy destroy my life, and I hate feeling like I'm still trying to recover."

"You weren't weak," Ashlyn says. "That was legitimately awful. No one would have gone through that unscathed."

"Maybe," I say. "But here I am, spending all this time with him, again. The man who tore me to pieces. I still wonder, every day, if today is the day I'll wake up and find out he's gone. He won't answer my calls and I'll go to his house and find it empty."

Gabe sips his wine, but doesn't say anything.

"Has he said anything that makes you think he'll take off?" Ashlyn asks.

"No," I say. "I just can't get past the fear that he will."

"What happened today?" Gabe asks. "You're not in there dumping your clothes out of the dresser because of a worry in the back of your mind."

"Dumping clothes out?" Ashlyn asks. "What?"

"I need to move out," I say. "I need to get out of this town."

"What happened?" Ashlyn, shifting to face me.

I tell them about Isaac, and Elaine, and how Hunter wants to get custody. "So, there I am, standing on his doorstep, and he tells me I shouldn't stay over. That he can't let me get close to Isaac unless I commit to him. What am I supposed to do with that?"

"Damn," Ashlyn says. "That's a lot to drop in your lap with no warning. What the hell are you supposed to do? Run off to the courthouse to get married so the kid doesn't get the wrong idea when you come out in the morning dressed in one of his shirts?"

"Exactly," I say.

"He was right," Gabe says quietly.

"Excuse me?" Ashlyn asks. "He was right to break up with Emma—again—because he's taking care of a kid? Lots of single parents date."

"He didn't break up with her," Gabe says. He meets my eyes. "Did he?"

"No, I'm the one who left," I say. "But he's asking me for a huge commitment. I'm not ready for that. I don't know if I ever will be."

"That's why he was right," Gabe says. "He knows you aren't ready, and he knows you might never get there. You sleep over at his house, but have you ever told someone you're anything other than friends? You keep him at a distance. Single parents can date, but I'm sure a lot of them are careful about introducing someone to their kid, let alone spending time all together."

I look down at my wine. I know Gabe is right. "Yeah, he said what happens if Isaac wakes up and we all have breakfast together, like I live there."

"Emma, I was just as skeptical about Hunter as you were," Gabe says. "I thought you were crazy when you told me you were seeing him again."

Ashlyn raises her hand. "Me, too."

"And I was proud of you for being careful," he says. "I don't want to see you get hurt again."

"But?" I ask.

"But, I think maybe I'm turning into a bitter old man before my time, and it's rubbing off on you," he says. "Why are you so convinced you can't have a relationship again?"

"Are you actually asking me that?" I ask. "I thought

Hunter and I were serious last time. I know we were young, but that didn't seem to matter back then. We felt so ... permanent. I really thought I was going to marry him, and then he left. I was devastated. But I moved on, and I made the mistake of letting someone in again. Wyatt made my life miserable for years, but I thought I had to make it work. That was marriage. And it's not like you've had it better than I have. You got married and that was a shit show. And look at Mom. She stayed with Dad through everything, and he took off. Relationships, marriage, none of it works for us."

"Wow, you really have made her bitter," Ashlyn says, looking at Gabe.

"I'm not bitter—and if I am, it isn't Gabe's fault," I say. "Point the finger at the assholes who broke my heart."

"Only one of those assholes actually broke your heart," Gabe says. "I don't think Wyatt really did."

"Yeah, the asshole who wants me to jump head first into his insta-family," I say.

"Look, I'm not saying you should," Gabe says. "If you don't want a relationship, then this shouldn't be a hard choice. He told you what he needs. You can't give it to him. You guys were just, what, kind of friends with benefits anyway, right?"

"No ... I..." I trail off, not sure what to say.

Gabe shrugs. "So, you were seeing each other almost every day. Going out and doing things together. Sleeping together at his house half the time. Not dating other people. But I guess that's not a relationship. That's what, banging your ex-boyfriend for a while?"

Ashlyn laughs so hard she snorts.

"Gabe!"

"Emma, you're so blind," he says. "You're all freaked out

because he wants a serious relationship, but you were already in one. You just didn't want to admit it."

"What happens if he flips out again?" I ask. "What happens if I give him what he wants, and we start building a life together, and then he bails?"

Gabe shrugs. "You just need to decide if he's worth the risk."

I put my glass down on the coffee table. "I don't know if anyone is worth that risk."

"Then I guess you have your answer," Gabe says.

## 24

## HUNTER

The coffee pot finishes brewing, and I pour a cup. Isaac isn't awake, so I don't need to be up. But I can't sleep late anyway. I was up half the night, tossing and turning, wondering if I did the right thing with Emma.

I pick up my notebook and turn to the page with my mission parameters. I was so sure when this started. I knew it wouldn't be easy; we had a lot of hurdles to overcome. But I thought if I did things right, I could show her. She'd learn to trust me again. She'd love me the way I've always loved her.

I haven't had enough time.

I could have let Emma stay with me last night. I missed her in my bed something fierce. She'd be here now, sipping coffee, waiting for Isaac to get up. We could take him to the park later, maybe go out for ice cream. She could come with us when we pick up his things from Elaine's. I think she would. Isaac took to her faster than I've seen him take to anyone, and I could see the feeling was mutual. She cared about him from the first time they met.

Emma's problem isn't that I'm taking on the responsibilities of a parent. The problem is me.

She doesn't trust me.

I don't know if she ever will. I've done everything I can to show her. I've tried to be patient, and give her what she needs. But the wounds I left were deep. Deeper than I can heal.

I grab a pen and scrawl one final note across the page before tossing it onto the kitchen counter. *Mission Failed.*

Isaac shuffles into the kitchen, carrying his Spiderman and sporting some epic bed head.

"Hey buddy," I say. "How did you sleep?"

He yawns. "Good."

I grab some cereal I have left from the last time he stayed over and pour him a bowl. "Want some breakfast?"

He nods and sits at the kitchen table.

I pour some milk and get him a spoon. "So, buddy, there's something I'd like to talk to you about." I set his breakfast in front of him and sit in the other chair.

He shovels a bite in his mouth and looks up at me.

"You know Grandma isn't feeling so well," I say. "She's pretty sick."

"I know," he says, his mouth full.

"I'm not sure how long she'll be in the hospital, but you're going to stay here, with me, okay?"

He nods and takes another bite.

"But I was thinking," I say. "What would you think about staying here all the time?"

He puts down his spoon. "You mean live here with you?"

"Yeah."

"Would I still see Grandma?"

"Yes, but it would be visits instead of living there," I say. "We'd go see her as often as we can. But we'd get all your clothes and toys and bring them here. You'd sleep here every night instead of just for sleepovers."

His big eyes brighten. "Really? Stay here all the time?"

"Yep, all the time. What do you think? Does that sound like a good idea?"

He gives me a big smile and my chest swells with emotion. "Yeah, I want to live here with you."

I swallow hard. "Good. You'll have to go to a new school, though. Is that okay too?"

"I'm only in kindergarten, Uncle Hunter," he says, his voice serious. "And I need you to teach me stuff."

"Yeah?" I ask. "What do you need me to teach you?"

"To use tools," he says, and takes another bite. "And how to be a gentleman."

Oh man, this kid. "Those are good things."

"And you can teach me to be a gentleman, right?" he asks. "Grandma says you can."

"I can definitely teach you to be a gentleman," I say. I reach across the table and ruffle his hair. "You're something else, you know that, buddy?"

He smiles and goes back to his breakfast.

WE PULL UP OUTSIDE MY PARENTS' house and I take a deep breath. I'm about to drop a fucking bomb in my mom's kitchen. My family knows about Isaac, and my mom has even met him a few times. She doted on him like he was her own grandson, even insisting he call her Grandma Maureen.

But hanging out with Isaac a few times a month, and raising him as my own, are two very different things. I hope they're on board with this. If I've ever needed my family's support, it's now.

I help Isaac out of the car. He wants me to carry him inside, so I do, holding him up with one arm.

"Will there be cookies?" Isaac asks when we get to the front door.

"There's a good chance," I say with a laugh. "Grandma Maureen usually has cookies."

I knock a couple times and push open the door. "Mom?"

"Is that you, Hunter?" Mom asks.

She's sitting in an armchair in front of the big fireplace, a book in her hand. She takes off her reading glasses and smiles at Isaac.

"Hi, Mom," I say.

Isaac buries his face in my neck.

"It's okay, you know Grandma Maureen," I say.

"I know what you need," Mom says, getting up from her chair. "Cookies."

"See?" I say, poking Isaac in the back until he squirms.

"Come on over to the table," Mom says. "Do you want some milk too, Isaac?"

"Yes," he says.

"Yes, what?" I ask.

"Yes, please," he says.

Mom smiles and pats him on the back as she walks by. She gets out a plate of cookies and sets them on the table, along with a small glass of milk. I put Isaac down and grab a cookie for myself.

"So what are you two boys up to today?" Mom asks.

"I live at Uncle Hunter's house now," Isaac says, his voice matter-of-fact.

Mom raises her eyebrows. "What's this?"

"Um, yeah," I say.

My dad comes down the stairs before I can say any more. "Hunter," he says to me with a nod. "Isaac, how are you, little man?"

Isaac tries to hide behind his cookie. "Hi, Papa Ed."

"Ed, maybe you could take Isaac down to the beach," Mom says. "We'll join you in a minute." She gives Dad a knowing look.

"We'll bring some cookies with us," Dad says, grabbing a handful. "Come on, kiddo."

Isaac jumps down from his seat and Dad takes him out the back door, closing it behind them.

Mom turns her interrogation face on me. "Hunter? What's going on?"

I take a seat at the dining table, and Mom follows, sitting across from me.

"Elaine was rushed to the hospital yesterday," I say. "I picked up Isaac, and I'm not sure how long she's going to be there."

"So Isaac just meant he's staying with you while his grandma is in the hospital," Mom says.

"Well, no," I say. "Actually, Isaac meant he's coming to live with me. Full time. I didn't think he was going to blurt it out like that."

Mom's eyes widen and her mouth hangs open for a moment. "Are you serious?"

I nod. "Very serious. Elaine's health is getting worse. She can't keep up with him now. Imagine in a few years. I've known this was coming for a while, and I've talked to Elaine about it several times. Isaac is coming to live with me. He needs someone to step in and be his family."

Mom puts a hand to her mouth and her eyes glisten with tears. "Oh, Hunter."

"He's so much like me," I say, looking down at the table.

"You guys gave me a chance. You gave me a home and a family. I can do that for him."

"Of course you can," she says, putting her hand on mine.

"I know this is a big deal," I say. "It's going to change everything. I have to get him registered for school, and figure out childcare when I have to work. It's ... I don't know, Mom, it's crazy. But I know it's the right thing to do."

"It *is* the right thing," Mom says, and a few tears run down her cheeks. "I'm so proud of you, son."

I meet her eyes. My throat feels thick, and I swallow hard.

"Well," she says, wiping her tears. "I can watch him anytime you need, so don't ever hesitate to ask. Have your brothers met him yet? I need to have everyone over for dinner."

I laugh. Of course she wants to feed everyone. "No, Cody and Ryan haven't met him yet. He's really shy around strangers, though, so maybe we can keep it mellow?"

She gets up from her seat and heads for the kitchen. "Of course we will. It's just dinner. Speaking of, have you had lunch yet?" She opens the fridge and starts pulling things out.

"Yeah, we ate before we came," I say.

"Do you have enough room at your house?" Mom asks.

"We can make it work, but I'm thinking I might need a bigger place," I say. "At least a place with a yard. I have an extra bedroom, but it would be nice if he had room to run around. He has a lot of energy."

"Boys do," Mom says. "And don't I know it. I raised three of you little terrors."

I laugh. "I know; we were a handful."

"What does Emma think of all this?" she asks.

Damn. I knew she'd ask about Emma, but part of me hoped she wouldn't. "Emma and I aren't really that serious."

"No?" she says. "I thought you were. You all went camping together."

"How do you know we went camping?" I ask, then realize what a stupid question that is. "Never mind. I'm sure Ryan or Cody told you."

"Nicole mentioned it, actually," she says. "It sounds like you all had a lot of fun."

"Yeah, it was fun," I say. Some parts more than others, but I'm not about to tell my mom those details. "But Emma's not ready for a commitment. At least, not to me."

"Why not?" Mom asks.

"Mom…" I pause. I've apologized to my parents numerous times for how I left, but I still don't like revisiting it. "I hurt her deeply when I left her. She doesn't know if she can trust me again."

Mom comes back to sit beside me.

"Honey, you're a good man," she says. "You're as good as they come. Emma loved you the way only an innocent heart can. That's a fragile thing. It's easily broken, and very hard to mend."

"It's impossible to mend."

"No, not impossible," she says. "If anyone can, it's you."

"I don't think so, Mom," I say. "Believe me, I tried."

Mom puts her hand on mine again. "Did you tell her the truth?"

"The truth?" I ask. "About what?"

"Why you left?"

I pull my hand away and look out the window. The tall dune grasses blow in the wind, and I can just see my dad and Isaac, walking toward the water. I don't want to talk to my mom about *why*. Not the real reason. I've done everything I can to apologize and make it right with my family, but there are some things I simply can't tell them.

"I told her how sorry I am," I say.

"That's a start," Mom says, her voice quiet. "But for her to trust you, she might need to hear the truth. All of it."

"The truth will make things worse," I say.

"It could," she says. "Sometimes the truth does unexpected things."

I nod, but the thought of telling Emma the truth about why I left ties my stomach in a knot. It isn't something I want to tell anyone.

I never have.

## 25

## EMMA

*T*he stack of flattened boxes tips precariously as I walk out of the hardware store. Gabe's friend John works there, and he said they had some boxes I could pick up for free. I don't need many; most of my stuff is still stacked in Gabe's garage. But a few more boxes will make moving a lot easier.

I found an apartment an hour and a half away. I keep thinking about relocating farther away—another state, even. I can work from anywhere. And in six months when my new lease is up, I just might. But I decided to chill out and not move too far away without a plan.

As it is, I took on a few freelance editing jobs and paid off my lawyer, so I'm free to go where I want. There's nothing keeping me at Gabe's house, and certainly nothing keeping me in Jetty Beach.

I wobble as I try to get my trunk open without dropping the boxes. I shove them inside and close the trunk, taking a deep breath. The air is cold, but it's a clear day. I'm supposed to meet Ashlyn for coffee in half an hour, so I have a little time to kill. I'm about to get in my car when something across the street catches my eye.

There's a little city park, with a circle of grass and a playground in the center. Hunter stands behind the swingset, pushing Isaac on the swing.

My heart leaps into my throat. I haven't seen Hunter in weeks. I've thought about calling him, but every time I reach for my phone, I stop. He wants something I can't give him, and I figure it's worse to let it drag out. We both need to move on.

But seeing him standing there, his strong arms gently pushing Isaac each time he swings back and forth, I can't get in my car.

I watch them for a few minutes. I don't think he realizes I'm here. He might have noticed my car, but his attention is entirely focused on Isaac. He walks around in front of him, saying something I can't hear—I think he's showing Isaac how to move his legs to swing by himself. Isaac slows down, but pumps his legs back and forth and starts going higher. Hunter claps, a wide smile on his face.

God, he's beautiful. He's thick, his body knotted with muscle, his arms covered with tattoos. He looks hard. Tough. He looks like a Marine.

But when he smiles at that little boy, it takes my breath away.

Before I realize what I'm doing, I cross the street and walk toward them. Hunter sees me and his brow furrows. The smile he gives me looks purposeful—genuine, but forced.

"Hi," he says.

"Hi." Shit, now I'm not sure what to say. "Sorry, I just saw you guys over here and thought I'd come say hello."

"Hi, Emma!" Isaac says, his voice bright. "I can swing by myself now."

"Wow, look at you," I say. "That's awesome."

I glance at Hunter, but he stands still, facing Isaac. We lapse into silence and I start to regret coming over. He clearly doesn't want to talk to me. I open my mouth to say goodbye, when he finally speaks.

"I left because I thought I had to," Hunter says.

My breath catches. "What?"

"After high school," he says. "I thought I had to protect you."

"From what?"

"From me."

I look over at him. He's standing with his hands in his pockets. Sunglasses cover his eyes, so I can't read his expression.

"What are you talking about?" I ask.

"I was an angry kid," he says. "You know that. What you don't know is that I had more than a bad temper. When I got mad, I imagined doing things to people. Terrible things. The things I'd see were so vivid—stronger than real memories. Sometimes I'd wake up in the morning and have to ask myself whether I shot our math teacher in the face the day before, because I could see it so clearly."

I'm not sure what to say, so I let him keep talking. Isaac leans back and forth, taking the swing higher.

"I don't know where it came from," he continues. "Maybe it was my dad leaving, or my mother being so busy I never saw her. It got worse when she died. The Jacobsens did what they could for me, and sports gave me an outlet. But I never talked about what I saw in my head. By the time you and I were together, I was pretty controlled. I didn't get in as many fights and I kept things locked down most of the time. But I was starting to wonder if I was some sort of monster, deep down. I still saw things in my mind, and I knew there was something in me that was capable of doing them. A part of me wanted to do them. I wanted to unleash all that rage and just ... I wanted to kill someone."

My stomach turns over.

"Not long before graduation, you and I got in an argument," he says. "I don't know what it was about. Probably something stupid. I was furious, and out of nowhere, I could see it all." He pauses and takes a deep breath. "I saw what I could do to you. The bruises on your face from where I hit you. Your lip split open. Blood dripping down your chin. I could feel your bones breaking against my hand. It was so goddamn real."

I put a hand to my mouth and look at Hunter out of the corner of my eye. He's looking straight ahead.

"I had never seen you that way before," he says. "Never. You were the only one. The only one I couldn't imagine hurting. So when I did see it, I realized you weren't safe from me. And if you weren't safe, no one was. Not my family, not my friends, no one. If I stayed, I was afraid one day I'd do it. I'd act on the things I saw in my head. I couldn't let that happen."

I swallow hard. "You never would have hurt me."

"No?" he asks. "I've done some of the things I used to imagine. To real people."

He's quiet for a moment and I try to process what he's telling me.

"In the Marines, I finally felt like I wasn't a monster," he says. "Maybe that was why I had all that rage burning inside me. I could use it. I was good at what I did. More than good. I rose fast. I carried out missions in some of the most dangerous places on earth. I was efficient, and very effective.

Everything I did, every confirmed kill, told me I made the right call. I was where I was supposed to be. I was made for it. I could serve my country, and protect the people I loved. And you were all safe from me."

"Then why did you come back?" I ask, my voice quiet.

"Somewhere along the way, the rage went away," he says. "I stopped seeing red when I got riled up. I stopped imagining hurting people. I stopped feeling so angry all the time. I don't know if I burned it all away or what. By the time I got in that accident, I could already see what was coming. And when I woke up, I knew it was time. I knew I could come home."

He takes a deep breath. "I don't regret leaving, Emma. I have to be honest about that. Maybe I never would have hurt you. But maybe I would have. Either way, serving in the Marines was what I needed. It shaped me into the man I am now, and I can't regret that. I'm at peace, and I wasn't before. But I do regret the way I left."

"Why did you do it?" I ask. "Why did you leave without telling me?"

"I was afraid," he says. "If I looked at you and told you I was leaving, and I couldn't let you follow, you would have tried to stop me. I didn't think I was strong enough to go if I faced you first. I was a scared kid. I hurt a lot of people that I love, and I'll always be sorry for that. Especially because of how badly I hurt you."

He stops and we stand in silence for a while, watching Isaac swing.

"I've never told anyone about the things I used to see," he says, his voice quiet. "This is the first time I've said it out loud. I even saw a therapist for a while, and I couldn't bring myself to tell her." He pauses again, taking a deep breath. "I didn't tell you why I left because I didn't want you to know this about me. You're going to look at me differently, and I wanted to avoid that. But you deserve the truth. And right now, I need you to know something. That rage and violence that was inside me is gone. No one needs to be afraid of me. Especially you."

"I'm not afraid of you," I say. "I never was."

"Yes, you are," he says. "You're afraid I'll leave you again. But I think—more than that—you're afraid I won't. You've been torn apart, but you're holding the shreds of yourself in such a tight grip that you won't let anyone else help stitch you back together."

I cross my arms and look away. I'm spared having to answer by Isaac, who jumps off the swing and comes barreling into Hunter's legs.

"I'm hungry," he says. "Can we get a snack?"

Hunter ruffles his hair. "Sure, bud. Why don't you say goodbye to Emma?"

He smiles. "Can you come with us, Emma?"

I swallow hard. "No, I'm sorry, I can't."

"Okay," he says. "Did you know I'm in kindergarten?"

I can't help but laugh. "Yes, you are. You're a big boy, now, aren't you?"

"Yep," he says.

He steps closer to me and opens his arms. "Bye, Emma."

I crouch down and he hugs me tight around the neck. Tears burn my eyes as I hug him back. "Bye, buddy."

I stand and bite the inside of my lip so I won't cry.

Hunter takes off his sunglasses and meets my eyes. "Bye, Emma. It was good to see you."

He picks up Isaac, and I watch them walk toward Hunter's truck.

I cross the street and get in my car. I lean my head back against the seat, my mind reeling. All this time, I wanted to understand why. Why did he leave the way he did? Why did he disappear?

I always thought it was because of me.

I blamed myself. I must have been too clingy. Too needy. We lived in a small town, and he felt trapped here with me. So he took off.

After all, he left a note for his parents. Me? Nothing. Not a word. So it had to have been my fault.

But it wasn't because of me. It was because he was afraid of hurting me. And I know he's telling the truth.

I could hear it in his voice, but more than that, I remember. I remember the argument he was talking about, and I remember how he looked at me that day. Something had changed. I saw fear in his eyes. I always thought he was afraid he'd gotten himself in too deep, that our relationship was too much for him at such a young age and he didn't know what to do to get out.

He wasn't afraid of *us*. He was afraid of *himself*.

His words echo in my memory. *The bruises on your face from where I hit you. Your lip split open. Blood dripping down your chin.* Could he have done that to me? Was he actually dangerous?

It's hard to know. I was never afraid of him in high school. Other people were, a few with good reason—but he was always gentle with me, even when we argued.

But *he* believed he was dangerous. In his mind, he was capable of hurting me. And he didn't want me to know. He didn't want me to be afraid.

I am afraid. He's absolutely right. Now I'm the one who's scared. He sees right through me. But I'm not afraid he'll be violent with me. I'm afraid of letting him in, afraid of losing myself and being in a position where someone can hurt me again.

As I drive home I realize that if I could let anyone in again, it would be him. It would be Hunter. He's already a part of me. He always was. That's why it was so hard when he left. He took a piece of me with him and he still has it. If I take the risk, I might feel whole again.

But I honestly don't know if I can.

## 26

## EMMA

*I* stare into the mostly-empty fridge, my stomach growling. Gabe almost never cooks at home, and neither of us have been to the store in a while. There are a handful of ingredients, but my choices are pretty limited, and I don't really feel like cooking. I have a standing invite to come up to Gabe's restaurant and haven't taken him up on it in a while, but tonight, a gourmet meal sounds pretty damn good. I throw on my coat, grab my purse, and head out the door.

My new apartment won't be ready for another week. I haven't admitted it to Gabe, but I'm having second thoughts. I even stopped by Hunter's house earlier today, thinking I might talk to him. What I would say, I still don't know. He's like a magnet, constantly tugging at me. I feel his pull wherever I go. But he wasn't home. I decided I shouldn't have stopped there anyway, and left.

The drive to Gabe's restaurant takes about twenty minutes. The parking lot is almost empty. It's late enough in the year that the tourist season has wound down, and the restaurant isn't very busy. I park and head inside.

A young man dressed in a black button down shirt leans against the host station, glancing up when I walk in. I think for a second, trying to remember his name.

"Good evening," he says.

"Samuel?" I ask.

"Yep," he says. "Emma, right? Are you here to see Gabriel, or do you want a table?"

"Both, I suppose."

"No problem," he says, and leads me to a table by the window.

There are a couple other patrons, but they're on the other side of the restaurant. Candles flicker in the center of the tables, reflecting off the wine glasses set at each place. Samuel takes my coat and pulls out my chair.

"I'll tell Gabriel you're here," he says.

"Thanks."

He didn't leave me with a menu, but they never do. Gabe always serves me what he feels like cooking when I stop by. I never complain. I have yet to taste something that isn't incredible.

I sit for a while, watching the waves crash against the sand. The restaurant is built on a hill overlooking the beach, and a spotlight illuminates the water at night.

"Hey, Emma."

I look over to find Clover approaching my table, two plates in her hands. She's dressed in a chef's coat with her name stitched on the front, and her curly hair is pulled back.

"Hi," I say.

"Mind if I join you?"

"No, not at all."

"Thanks." She smiles, setting the plates on the table, and takes the seat across from me. "It's really slow tonight.

Gabriel just has me testing out new recipes. He said you were here, so I figured I'd come say hi."

"Did you make this?" I ask, gesturing to my plate. It's salmon with a side of roasted root vegetables.

"I did," she says, her voice bright. "It's just something I was trying out. If you hate it, I can get you something else."

I cut into the salmon and take a bite. It's heavenly. "No, this is wonderful."

"Yeah?" she asks. "Good. I'm glad you were here. I like being able to try things out on someone other than Gabriel."

"It's amazing," I say.

We both start eating and a few minutes pass in silence.

"So, do you want to talk about him?" she asks.

"Hunter?" I ask. "There's not much to talk about."

"It's okay if you don't," she says, and takes another bite. "He misses you, though."

I'm not sure what to say, so I keep eating.

"Isaac is the best, isn't he?" she asks. "Maureen's going nuts over the whole thing. She and Ed are watching Isaac, since Hunter had to go out of town. She's going to stuff that kid so full of sugar."

I shouldn't ask, but I can't help it. "Hunter's out of town?"

"Yeah, he had to go see some big shot client on the east coast or something," she says. "I don't know, he never tells anyone what he's really doing. I guess he can't, which is so freaking cool. He's such a badass. Anyway, he left this afternoon. Cody and I are taking Isaac tomorrow night. I can't wait. It's the perfect excuse to watch kid movies."

My shoulders tense up at the thought of Hunter leaving town. Logically, I know it's just a business trip. He told me he has to go out of town occasionally. But knowing he left leaves me feeling unsettled.

Clover's phone buzzes and she pulls it out of a pocket. "Sorry, it's Cody. Do you mind if I take this really quick?"

"No, not at all," I say.

"Hey, sexy man," she says with a smile, but instantly her face drops. "What? Oh my god." Her eyes widen with alarm. "Is he okay? Yeah, I can leave. I'll meet you there." She hangs up and stands. "Isaac got hurt and they're at the hospital. I'm sorry, I have to go."

My breath catches in my throat and I stand up. "I'll come."

We rush out to Clover's car and I get in, my heart racing. Cody's a doctor; if they're taking Isaac to the hospital, it must be something he can't handle at his clinic. "Did Cody say what happened?"

Clover pulls out onto the highway. "No, but he sounded like he was in a hurry."

I clutch my purse and stare out the window while Clover drives. A million scenarios run through my mind, each one worse than the last. He fell and cut his head open. He broke his leg. What if it's more serious than that? He must be so scared, especially because Hunter isn't here.

We get to the hospital and Clover checks her phone. "He's in the children's ward."

Inside, we head for the elevators. The children's ward is on the third floor, and the stupid elevator will not move fast enough. I tap my foot and chew on my lower lip. I think about calling Hunter, but I'm sure someone already did.

The elevator doors open and Clover rushes up to a nurse's station. "We're looking for Isaac Lynch."

"Room three-ten," the nurse says, pointing down the hall to the left.

We find the room, but it's empty.

"What the hell?" Clover says. She pokes her head back

into the hallway. "Excuse me? We're missing a kid over here."

A guy in blue scrubs stops. "Can I help you?"

I step forward. "We're looking for a patient, Isaac Lynch. We were told he was in this room."

The nurse turns and consults a white board. "Looks like he was taken in for surgery."

"Surgery!" Clover says.

"Do you know where the rest of his family is?" I ask.

"Probably the surgical waiting room," he says. "I can show you."

The nurse leads us down a hallway and through a set of double doors. We round a corner and find the whole Jacobsen family: Ed and Maureen, Ryan and Nicole, and Cody. Cody walks forward and hugs Clover.

"What happened?" I ask.

"He fell down the stairs," Cody says. His voice is calm, but I can see the concern in his eyes. "Compound fracture of both the radius and ulna, and a dislocated elbow. Essentially, he snapped his forearm half. He also has a gash on his forehead that will need stitches."

"Oh my god," I say. "He's in surgery already?"

Cody nods. "I called a friend of mine. He's the best pediatric surgeon I know. He came right down."

I put a hand to my chest. I'm so overwhelmed, I don't know what to do. "How long will he be in surgery?"

"We should be able to see him in a couple hours," Cody says.

My eyes burn with tears. "He must have been terrified."

"He was a tough little guy," Cody says. "For as much pain as he must have been in, he handled it really well. We made sure he didn't get a good look at his arm. It was pretty bad."

Cody puts his arm around Clover and he leads her to a

seat near his parents. Ed sits next to Maureen, his hand on her shoulder while she clasps her hands in her lap. Her face is lined with worry. Ryan paces up and down, his hands in his pockets, and Nicole sits nearby.

I take a seat and try not to fidget too much. I keep glancing up at the door, and at the clock.

After what feels like an eternity, a doctor comes in and everyone stands up. He shakes hands with Cody.

"How is he?" Cody asks.

"He did very well," the doctor says. "I set the bone, and he needed three pins to keep it in place. Those will come out in about six weeks. His forehead definitely needed stitches. But he's young. It will heal up so well that he might not even have a scar."

"Thank you," Cody says. "When can we see him?"

"He's still waking up," the doctor says. "But I can bring one or two of you back now."

"Great. Mom, how about you and I go see him first."

Maureen gets up, and she and Cody follow the surgeon through the double doors.

I sit back down and wait, wishing I could have been the one to go back first. I'm overwhelmed with the desire to be there when he wakes up. Which doesn't make sense. These people are his family now. They should be the ones taking care of him. But I can't get the image of his little broken body lying at the bottom of the stairs out of my mind. I need to see his face. I need to see that he's okay.

After a while, Cody and Maureen come out.

"He's sleeping," Cody says. "Mom hasn't eaten, so maybe we should all get some food. He'll be pretty sleepy for a while."

Everyone gets up and moves toward the elevator. I'm not

sure if I should follow. I clutch at my purse, feeling awkward.

"Do you want to go see him?" Cody asks, his voice quiet.

"Can I?" I ask.

He nods. "Yeah. I'll take you back." He turns to Clover. "I'll catch up with you."

I follow Cody through the doors and down a long hallway. He brings me into a wide room and pulls back a blue curtain.

Isaac is on a bed with metal rails on both sides. His left arm is bent at the elbow, with a cast that goes almost to his shoulder, and his forehead has a bandage over it. His little fingers twitch, and his eyes are closed.

Cody gives me a small smile. "He's pretty groggy. He might not wake up for a while."

"Okay."

I pull up a chair next to the bed. One of his feet is sticking out of the bottom of the blanket, so I cover it back up again. I put my hand on his leg and watch him breathe.

Footsteps approach behind me and I hear the curtain draw back. "Emma?"

I gasp at Hunter's voice.

He comes around to the other side of the bed. "Do you know what happened? They said he fell down the stairs?"

"That's what Cody said. He had a compound fracture and he needed stitches in his forehead."

Hunter stares at Isaac, his brow furrowed, and places a gentle hand on Isaac's chest. "Fuck, I can't believe this happened."

"I thought you were gone," I say.

He looks up at me. "I was. I was at the airport, waiting to board my flight. Cody called and I came back as fast as I could." He scoots a stool over so he can sit down and takes

Isaac's other hand in his. "Damn it, buddy. I'm so sorry I wasn't here."

I can't help but stare at Hunter, and the tears that have been threatening to spill over for the last few hours finally do.

He's here. I've been so afraid to believe Hunter had it in him to stay, I've done nothing but push him away. Every time he tried to get close, I balked. He was so patient with me. So careful. After all that we've been through, he gave me every chance to see the man he's become. And I was too clouded by fear to see him clearly.

I see him now.

I see a man who's willing to give up everything for someone else, who's so committed to becoming a father to a child who isn't his own that he's making what must be agonizing choices, and putting Isaac first.

I swipe my fingers across my cheeks, hoping Hunter doesn't notice. "Well, I'm glad you were able to get here. I'm sure he'll be fine, but he'll be glad to see you when he wakes up."

Hunter looks at me again, like he's only just now seeing me. "How did you know?"

"I was at the restaurant with Clover when Cody called," I say.

"And you came?"

"Yeah," I say. "I didn't know what happened or if he was okay. And Clover said you were out of town on business. I guess it was silly of me to come, though. Of course your whole family would be here. It's not like Isaac needed another person to sit in the waiting room."

I stand, suddenly overwhelmed. Here I am, intruding on this intensely personal moment that I have no right to see. I shouldn't have come.

"I'm sorry, I should go."

I turn and move the curtain aside.

"Emma," Hunter says.

I glance over my shoulder.

"Thank you for coming," he says. "It's good to see you."

I nod. "You too."

I walk back down the hallway, fighting back tears. I make it as far as the elevator when I stop in my tracks.

*It's good to see you.*

Every time we see each other, Hunter says those words. My breath catches and my chest feels tight. Holy shit, he's been pulling a *Princess Bride* on me this entire time. He hasn't been saying *It's good to see you*. He's been saying *I love you*.

And now I'm the one leaving. I'm the one trying to disappear.

I turn around and rush back to the recovery room. Isaac is still asleep, Hunter's big hand holding his small one. Hunter's eyes lift when I come around the curtain.

"I love you, too," I say. His mouth drops open, and I have no idea what I'm saying, but I plow ahead anyway. "You've been trying to tell me you love me from day one, haven't you? It's okay that you didn't say it. You were probably afraid of pushing me away. But I felt it. I felt it every time we were together and it scared the shit out of me. How could you love me? If you'd loved me ten years ago, you wouldn't have left. But you did love me then, and you still do now, and goddamn it Hunter, I love you too. I'm so scared, but I'm an idiot for denying it for so long. I'm so sorry." I stop and take a trembling breath. "I want in, Hunter. I love you and I want this. I want you, and Isaac. I'm so terrified I can barely breathe, but the only thing that scares me more than this is the thought of losing you forever."

I wait a beat for the crash. He's going to tell me it's too late—he's sorry, but I lost my chance.

Instead, he surges around the bed and wraps me in his thick arms. "I do love you," he says, his voice low. "I never stopped. Not for a moment."

I wrap my arms around his neck, holding him tight. He's solid and steady. "I'm sorry I've been so difficult."

"You haven't," he says. "You're worth it, Emma. You're worth everything."

I lift my face, eyes drifting closed, and his mouth finds mine. His lips feel exquisite. He holds me tight, pressing my body against his, kissing me softly.

"Uncle Hunter?"

He breaks the kiss and moves to the side of the bed.

"Hi, buddy," he says.

Isaac blinks hard. "I fell down the stairs."

"I know, bud," he says. "You're going to be okay."

Isaac nods and his eyes start to close again.

"Just rest," Hunter says. "I'm here."

"Is that Emma?" Isaac asks. He doesn't open his eyes.

I come closer and touch his hand. "Yeah, sweetie. It's Emma."

"Good," he says. He squeezes my fingers and lets out a little sigh.

# EPILOGUE

HUNTER

*E*mma stands in the kitchen with her hands on her hips. The cupboards are all open and she's surrounded by half-unpacked boxes. Stacks of plates, glasses, pots, pans, and mugs cover the counters. I walk up behind her and slip my hands around her waist.

"Why don't you leave this for now?" I say, and trail a line of kisses down her neck.

"I can't just leave it," she says. "We need a functional kitchen. It's one of those things you have to do when you move. Beds to sleep in. A kitchen to cook in. The rest of the unpacking is what can wait."

We got a house on the same street as Cody and Clover's. It's a two story with three bedrooms upstairs and a big back-yard. I already have plans to build a playset in the back for Isaac.

I wrap Emma's ponytail around my hand and gently pull her head to the side. I slide my tongue across her skin, from her shoulder up to her ear, then nip her earlobe with my teeth.

"Take a little break," I say. "I'll help you later." I reach around to cup her breast and kiss harder down her neck.

She sighs, her body relaxing into me. "We need to be able to make breakfast tomorrow."

"I'll make breakfast," I say into her ear. "Come upstairs and help me make the bed."

"We have that thing at Isaac's school. And you already made the bed."

I spin her around and kiss her mouth, firm and demanding. "Then help me mess it up. We have time."

She nods, her eyes half closed. I take her upstairs into the master bedroom, and close the door.

We're undressed in seconds, falling onto the bed in a tangle. I grab her hips and thrust my cock inside her, moaning into her neck. Her body yields to mine. She's hot, breathless. I love making her feel this way. I could do this forever.

I take us both to the brink and slow down. I want to stretch this out, savor every moment, every movement, every sensation. She feels better than anything I can imagine. When I speed up, thrusting into her harder, she calls my name. Her pussy clenches, so hot, throbbing around me, and I'm undone. I pour myself into her, coming with fury, with passion, with intensity that drowns out the world.

When we both finish, I lie next to her. She rests her head on my shoulder as we both catch our breath.

"There's a little something I need to talk to you about," she says, running a finger down my chest.

"Yeah?"

"Although, things have been so hectic lately, with the move and everything," she says. "Maybe this isn't the best time to bring it up."

I prop my head up on my hand so I can look at her. "It's okay, Ems. What do you need to talk about?"

"Well, I know we haven't really discussed having a baby yet—"

"Wait." I put a finger to her lips. A jolt of adrenaline runs through me, making my limbs tingle. "You want to have a baby with me?"

"Well, yeah—"

I shouldn't keep interrupting, but I can't help kissing her. I put my hand alongside her face and caress her lips with mine. I need a moment before I can speak again.

My mind is reeling. We've been living together for months, but I haven't proposed yet. She moved into my old place with me and Isaac just a few days after his surgery. And even though tonight will be our first night in this house, it already feels like home. It's our home. Our family. The three of us.

And we can make it four.

I kiss her again to buy time. This isn't what I was planning, but maybe it's the right moment. I've had her ring for a week.

Should I give it to her now?

It's in my coat pocket, downstairs. I check a hundred times a day to make sure I haven't lost it. If I get up to get it now, the moment might be lost. But I could ask her without it, and tell her I have it. This isn't the grand proposal I was envisioning, but she just said one of the most amazing things anyone has ever said to me in my entire life.

"Are you okay?" she asks when I pull away.

"Yeah, I'm sorry. That made my heart race a little. But I really, really want to have a baby with you."

"You do?"

"Definitely." She smiles and I know it's time. I swallow hard, my heart pounding. "Emma—"

My phone rings.

*Shit.*

I think about ignoring it, but Isaac is at school. I should at least check.

"Hold that thought," I say.

I grab my phone, but it isn't the school. It's my mom. I roll my eyes, but decide to answer. "Hi, Mom."

"Hunter, are you and Emma coming to Isaac's school?" she asks.

"Yes, we'll be there," I say. "Why? Wait, what time is it?"

"It starts in five minutes," she says.

Oops. I guess my little diversion took longer than I thought. "Damn it. Sorry, Mom. Yeah, we'll be right there." I hang up. "We're late."

Emma and I throw the covers back and jump out of bed. I yank on a pair of jeans and a dark green shirt while Emma runs into the bathroom. A few minutes later, she comes out wearing a long striped dress with a little white sweater, her long hair hanging down around her face.

"You look beautiful," I say.

She smiles. "Let's go."

We drive to Isaac's school and find a spot among the other cars. It's the end of the school year, and the kindergarten is putting on a program. Isaac has been practicing the song they're supposed to sing for the last several weeks, singing at the top of his lungs all day long.

We hurry inside to the gym. There's a stage set up with rows of chairs in front of it, and Isaac's class is already standing there. I see him on the end, his hair sticking up in the back. His arm healed well and there's only a hint of a scar on his forehead where he needed stitches. He sees me and grins, showing off his newly missing front teeth.

Emma and I find seats in the back. My mom and dad are already here, sitting near the front with Elaine. We moved Elaine to an assisted living home in Jetty Beach a few months ago, so she can get the care she needs, and see Isaac regularly. It's expensive, but it's worth every penny.

Isaac's teacher stands in front of the class and talks about the things they've learned this year. The kids fidget behind her until it's time for them to sing their song. Isaac belts out the words proudly, along with the rest of his class. It's hard to believe he's the same shy little guy who came to live with me. He's done well in school and made friends. He's still a bundle of energy, but Emma and I do our best to give him a lot of time to run around.

I glance over at Emma, and my mind is filled with thoughts of growing our family. Isaac is going to love being a big brother. It makes me want to gather her up in my arms and kiss her until neither of us can breathe. But we're in a gym full of people, so I settle for grabbing her hand and twining my fingers through hers.

After the program, Mom insists we all go out for an early dinner. Emma and I are still getting our stuff moved into the new house, and would have probably grabbed takeout anyway, so I agree. I stick my hand in my pocket on the way out to my truck, feeling the box I've been carrying around with me. I keep thinking I'll find the perfect moment, the perfect words. I was so close before my mom called— although I'm glad she did. I would have felt terrible if we'd missed Isaac's program.

I'm distracted through dinner. I'm grateful Emma asks for a table with a wall behind us so I don't have to sit with people walking behind me. It isn't always a problem, but I'm already edgy. I feel like everyone can see the truth written all over my face. Emma asks me several times if I'm okay, and I assure her I'm fine. Mostly I just do my best to stay calm.

When we get home, Isaac wants to go outside and play. I make sure he keeps his coat on, and send him to the backyard. Emma goes into the kitchen to finish putting things away. I stand for a long moment, looking out the back door, fingering the box in my coat pocket.

"Are you staying?" Emma asks.

"What?"

"You're still wearing your coat."

I look down. "Oh, right."

Glasses clink as she starts putting them in a cupboard. "Were you going to say something before?"

"When?"

"Before your mom called earlier," she says. "I thought maybe there was something you were going to say."

I meet her eyes. She's so beautiful. She's the most beautiful woman I've ever known.

"Are you okay? You're kind of worrying me," she says. "You seem tense."

"No, I'm fine." I walk over to her and brush my fingers across her lips. I take her hand and hold it against my chest. I'm flying blind here, no mission parameters to guide me, but I know it's time. "I did have something to say before. There's something I've been wanting to ask you."

Her lips part and her eyebrows lift. "Yes?"

"Emma, I was wondering ... will you marry me?"

She gasps and covers her mouth, tears springing to her eyes.

I reach into my pocket and bring out the box. "I've loved

you since we were kids, Ems. I want you to be with me, always."

I let go of her hand and open the box.

"Of course I'll marry you." She looks up and meets my eyes. "I thought you'd never ask."

I laugh. "I didn't want to risk asking you too soon." With careful fingers, I take the ring out of the box. A tear trails down her cheek as I slip it on her finger.

I pull her close and kiss her, taking in her scent, reveling in the feel of her against me. She threads her arms around my neck and I hold her tight, kissing her deeply.

"Should we tell Isaac?" I glance out the kitchen window. He's running around in the grass, pretending to beat up bad guys.

"Yeah," she says, swiping a tear from her cheek. "Although..."

"Is something wrong?"

"No, it's just that..." She pauses. "I was trying to tell you something before, but you wouldn't stop kissing me."

I smile and plant a kiss on her sweet lips. "It's hard. I love kissing you."

She laughs. "When we were talking earlier, I wasn't trying to ask you if you want to have a baby. I was trying to find the right moment to tell you that we're going to have a baby."

My heart thumps hard and instinctively, I draw her closer. "Emma, you're...?"

"Yes." She looks deep into my eyes. "I am. I'm pregnant with our baby."

I scoop her up in my arms, holding her tight against me, and close my eyes. I let her words sink in. She's everything I ever needed. I spent so long believing I'd lost her forever.

Now she's here, with me. In our home. Wearing my ring. Having my baby.

Mission accomplished.

READY FOR MORE HAPPILY EVER AFTERS IN Jetty Beach? Turn the page for a preview of Weekend Fling.

## WEEKEND FLING: CHAPTER 1

JULIET

*I* fall backward onto the bed with an exaggerated sigh. "You guys *have* to tell me what's going on. This is the worst."

Number of times I've begged my girlfriends to tell me what we're doing: eleven.

Becca throws a cardigan on top of my face. "Hush, you. We'll tell you when we're good and ready."

I groan and throw it back at her. She bats it down to the floor, and tucks her blond hair behind her ear before she goes back to packing my bag.

Number of times they've listened: zero.

"Calm your tits, Juliet," Madison says. Her curly brown hair is a little wild around her face, and she's wearing a t-shirt that says *the sass is strong with this one*. "We'll get you all packed, and then maybe we'll tell you where we're going."

It's like they don't know me *at all*. They show up at my house at seven on a Thursday morning, ambushing me before work. Then they tell me the three of us are going out of town for a long weekend, but they won't tell me where. They won't tell me *anything*.

Surprises are really not my thing. And they're doing this to me after I explicitly told them I want to let this weekend go by with absolutely no fanfare whatsoever. Nothing. Nada. I don't want to think about it. I don't want to talk about it. And I *really* don't want to fucking celebrate it.

But my friends Becca and Madison? Oh no, they couldn't let it go. They couldn't let a girl have a birthday in peace.

So here I am, lying on my bed while my girlfriends go through my closet, packing a bag for me. I'm itching—absolutely itching out of my skin—over this. I'm going to have to go through my bag before we leave, because I cannot go away for the weekend with a bag someone else packed. Are they kidding me with this scene? I keep packing lists handy, and they won't even *look* at them. As if they're going to know what I'll need to bring for a weekend away.

"This is the stupidest thing you two have ever done," I say.

"And you're being a whiny bitch," Madison says with a laugh. "We're trying to do something fun and nice for you, and all you're doing is complaining."

"Something nice?" I ask. "Something nice would be bringing me a bottle of vodka and leaving me alone with it so I can drown my old-lady sorrows."

Becca laughs. "Stop being such a drama queen. You're not old."

"I'm almost old," I say. "I will be on Saturday."

"If twenty-eight is old, then people are old for most of their lives," Madison says. "Birthdays are fun, and we aren't letting you get away with not celebrating."

"Fine, we can celebrate," I say. "But tell me what we're doing. You guys know how much I hate this."

"No, we are not telling you." Becca folds a skirt and puts it in my bag. "You need to loosen up. Like, a lot. We're going to show you that being spontaneous can be fun. Even if you think it's going to kill you. Which it won't."

I groan again. "Okay, don't tell me where we're going. But let me pack."

"You don't know what we're doing, so you don't know what to pack," Madison says. "Honestly, Jules, we've got this. Go downstairs and have some coffee. We'll finish up here and then we can head out."

"Ugh." I haul myself up off the bed. "Fine."

"Your latte is on the counter," Becca says. "Sixteen-ounce, two percent, one raw sugar, extra foam."

"Okay, maybe you do love me," I say, and head down the stairs.

Becca and Madison really are the best. I love them dearly, even when they piss me off. I just don't know why they're always insisting I go against my nature. I like to have things planned in advance. What's so bad about that? I'm organized and on top of things. I'm punctual and reliable. Those are good traits in a person. Yet they always insist I need to throw caution to the wind. Take risks. I take plenty of risks. Just last week I went to a restaurant I'd never been to, *and* I didn't have time to read the entire menu before I ordered. I just picked one of the first things I saw that looked good. Do they appreciate what it took for me to do that? Oh, no. Of course not. They call me an overthinking control freak.

I grab the coffee they brought and sit on the couch. It's my overthinking control-freak nature that's gotten me this far in life, so I don't see the problem. I own my own business, I bought this lovely townhouse last year, and I make enough money to indulge in cute clothes and pretty shoes when I want to. My life is just fine, thank you very much. I don't need them whisking me away for secret girls' week-ends for my birthday—with no information whatsoever.

"Jules," Madison yells down the stairs. "Where's your makeup bag?"

"Oh my god, at least let me pack my own bathroom shit," I yell at her.

"Just tell me where the bag is," she says. "It's not that hard."

"They're all in the second drawer, and everything is color-coded, so don't get it all mixed up!"

Madison doesn't answer. Yep, I'm going to have to repack, and they're going to whine at me for how long it's taking.

A few minutes later, Becca hauls my suitcase down the stairs.

I jump up from the couch. "Drop that right there. I need to go through it."

"Nope," she says with a big smile. "We're leaving. Right now."

"Just let me make sure nothing will get wrinkled," I say.

Madison appears behind me and grabs my shoulders, pointing me toward the front door. "Come on, Jules. Let's go."

Becca opens the door and carries my suitcase outside while Madison pushes me out. She grabs my purse on the way and hands it to me.

"Keys," Madison says. "Hand them over."

"What? Why?"

"Because I won't have you bolting back inside, or making a run for your car," she says. "I'll lock up."

I scowl at her and dig in my purse, finding my keys. I drop them into her outstretched palm with a clink.

"Thank you," she says.

I watch to make sure the door actually locks, then follow them to Madison's car.

Becca's putting my suitcase in the trunk, and I see there are two more suitcases already in there. I guess they're serious about going out of town.

"Birthday girl rides shotgun," Becca says and gets in the back.

"That's something, at least." I get in the passenger's seat and Madison goes around to the driver's side.

"Okay, girls," Madison says, starting up the engine. "Are you ready for an awesome fucking weekend?"

"Yes!" Becca says.

I raise my eyebrows. "Yay?"

Madison digs around in the center console. Her mess doesn't bother me because it isn't *my* mess, but I have no idea how she functions in this car. There's shit everywhere. Finally, she pulls out a plastic silver tiara with pink rhinestones.

"For the birthday princess," she says.

I laugh and put it on, then look in the mirror and smooth down my light brown hair. "Very sexy. Now will you tell me where we're going?"

"No."

I shake my head, but I smile. I can't stay mad at them. And the truth is, as uncomfortable as this spontaneous stuff makes me, I know we'll have a great time together. We always do.

Madison pulls out onto the street and heads for the freeway. Our direction will be my first clue, so I'm anxious to see which route she takes.

She pulls up to a stop sign and glances at me. "Do you want me to avoid going by his building?"

"No, I told you, I'm fine." By *his*, she means Jacob's place. My ex. Recent ex.

"Are you sure?" she asks. "I can avoid it."

"I'm sure. It honestly doesn't bother me." I'm not really telling the truth, and I can tell Madison knows it. But I don't want it to bother me, so I'm trying the *fake it till you make it* thing.

People saw me and Jacob as the perfect match. He's a lot like me, so it seemed like we'd be great together. He's organized, punctual, and driven. We both appreciate proper planning. Neither of us likes to make snap decisions, especially about things that are important. Our relationship had a level of structure that was comforting. I knew what I was getting with Jacob. There weren't any surprises.

Of course, no surprises got a little boring. He insisted on doing things the same way, every time. I like my routine, but Jacob was incapable of doing anything outside the norm. My friends say I'm set in my ways, but Jacob was a stone fucking statue who would not budge.

And life in the bedroom? My friends would never believe me, but I actually like spontaneity when it comes to sex. I like to mix it up and try new things. Jacob? Not so much. It was the same thing, every time. It wasn't awful, but there wasn't much to it, either.

We'd been dating for two years, and I kind of figured he was the one. He wasn't perfect, but hell, who is? We were comfortable together. And isn't that enough for a marriage? Comfort?

When he told me he thought we should break up, I was floored. It felt like it came out of nowhere, but looking back, I should have known. And as hurt as I was, it didn't take me long to realize it was probably for the best.

But now? I'm about to turn twenty-eight, and I'm starting

over. This is *not* where I planned to be at this age, and I think that, even more than losing Jacob, is what really pisses me off.

"Has it really only been a month since you guys broke up?" Becca asks.

"Yeah."

"Wow, it feels like it's been longer," she says. "You seem like you're so fine. A month after my last relationship ended, I was still in the 'eating ice cream for dinner' phase."

"I remember," I say. "It's hard, but I'm just trying to move on, you know?"

"Hey, maybe we'll meet some hot men this weekend," Madison says.

"Um, neither of you are meeting hot men," I say. "Last time I checked, I'm the only one of us who is pathetically single."

Madison stretches out her left hand and admires her engagement ring. "True, I am off the market, aren't I? But Becca, Brandon better put a ring on it soon, or you need to seriously consider your options."

"Stop," Becca says with a laugh. "You get engaged, and suddenly everyone needs a ring?"

"Oh, come on," Madison says. "You've been with Brandon for three fucking years. That guy needs to commit."

"He will when he's ready," Becca says. "I'm not rushing him."

"Whatever," Madison says. "Fine, I'm not looking for hot men, but if I find one for Juliet, I'm hooking a girl up."

I laugh. "That's fair. I am the birthday girl."

"That's the spirit," Madison says. She eyes me from the side. "You know what? That's what I want to get you for your birthday."

"What?" I ask.

"Laid."

I burst out laughing and have to readjust my tiara. "I seriously doubt you're getting me laid for my birthday."

"Why not?" she asks. "That would be the ultimate birthday present. If I can pull that off, I'm an uber-badass."

"If you get me laid this weekend, I'll buy you a medal that says *Best Fucking Friend in the Universe*," I say.

Becca laughs. "Right, like Juliet would sleep with a guy she just met."

"Oh, now the fact that I like to date men for a while before I let them get me naked is a bad thing?"

"No, I'm just saying sleeping with someone you just met would be way too spontaneous for you," Becca says.

"It would not."

Madison snorts. "Have you ever done it?"

"Have you?"

Madison glances at me with an eyebrow raised.

"Okay, I know you have," I say. "Becca?"

"All right, no," she says. "But neither have you."

"You're right, I've never done it," I say. "And no, I don't know if I ever would. You're probably right, that's way outside my comfort zone. But this magical hottie we're going to meet this weekend might make me change my mind."

Madison laughs. "If only. But we do have an awesome weekend planned, okay? We really wanted to surprise you and do something fun. You've been too pouty about your birthday this year, and I know the whole Jacob thing has been hard. This is going to be great."

I take a deep breath. "Okay, I'm sorry I was being a snot about it. I'll loosen up and we'll have so much fun."

"There you go," Madison says. Becca reaches forward and squeezes my shoulder.

"Now will you tell me where we're going?" I ask, noticing we're getting on the freeway heading south.

"No," they both say in unison.

I sigh and settle back into my seat, wondering what they have in store for me.

# AFTERWORD

Dear reader,

Maybe I tested Hunter's patience so much in this story because this book tested mine.

I knew I would write Hunter's story way back when I was writing the first Jetty Beach book. He comes home, reuniting with his adoptive family during Ryan and Nicole's story. From that point forward, his story swirled around in the back of my mind, and I was so excited to write it. But, I had to wait.

I love a good second chance romance. There are so many big feels when a couple has already been in love, and lived through hard times. And these two certainly had some hard times to get past.

If you've read my other novels, you probably already know what a soft spot I have for heroes who are Good Men. I think I write so many heroes that way because I love to celebrate the good men of the world. They're out there—I know quite a few of them. That isn't to say the characters I create aren't flawed—they are. But I love writing about men with big hearts who adore their women.

Hunter isn't perfect, but his heart is so very good. He's a protector. Even as a teenager, he had a desire to protect the people he loved. He didn't bail on his family because he was an asshole—he left because he thought he had to. He didn't think they were safe if he was around. Was that true? There's really no way to know. The important thing is that Hunter believed that, to his very core. And as he tells Emma late in the book, serving in the military wasn't a mistake for him. He needed something to help him work through his anger. By the time we meet him, he's a much calmer man than he would have been without his military service. Whether or not he would have been dangerous to the people he loved is hard to say, but the Hunter who returns home certainly isn't. He's found peace.

Although PTSD isn't the central theme of this book, Hunter does have some residual struggles with it. I didn't want that to overwhelm the story, but I also wanted to acknowledge that seeing combat changed him, and not all of those changes were positive.

I think the key to understanding Emma is something she realizes late in the story: Hunter took a piece of her with him when he left. She doesn't struggle to get over him for a decade simply because the way he left was traumatic. It was, certainly. Not knowing where he'd gone or what happened, or even whether he was alive, would have eaten a hole in anyone's heart. But it was deeper than that. He and Emma shared a powerful love at a young age, and when he left, Emma was no longer whole. She feels a certain amount of shame over the fact that ten years later, she's still hurt. But I don't see her as weak. She loved deeply at an age when many girls wouldn't be able to open their hearts to someone so fully. She was strong enough in herself to do so—to love

Hunter with a depth that transcended their young age. Unfortunately, she got hurt in the process.

But I think Hunter made up for it.

A quick note about Isaac. His name is a tribute to my older half-brother, who was born too early to stay in this world. With my mom's blessing, I used his name for the sweet little boy in this story.

I hope you enjoyed Hunter and Emma's story! Thanks for reading!

CK

# ALSO BY CLAIRE KINGSLEY

For a full, up-to-date listing of Claire Kingsley books visit
www.clairekingsleybooks.com

## The Jetty Beach Romance Series

Sexy small-town romance series with swoony heroes, romantic
HEAs, and lots of big feels.

Behind His Eyes

One Crazy Week

Messy Perfect Love

Operation Get Her Back

Weekend Fling

Good Girl Next Door

The Path to You

The Jetty Beach Box Set Books 1-4

## Bootleg Springs

### by Claire Kingsley and Lucy Score

Hot and hilarious small-town romcom series with a dash of
mystery and suspense.

Whiskey Chaser

Sidecar Crush

Moonshine Kiss

Bourbon Bliss

More Bootleg Springs coming in 2019

## The Miles Family Series

Sexy, sweet, funny, and heartfelt family series. Messy family. Epic bromance. Super romantic.

Broken Miles: Roland & Zoe

Forbidden Miles: Brynn & Chase

Reckless Miles: Cooper & Amelia

Hidden Miles: Leo & ?

Gaining Miles: A Miles Family Novella

## Remembering Ivy

A unique contemporary romance with a hint of mystery.

## His Heart

A poignant and emotionally intense story about grief, loss, and the transcendent power of love.

## Book Boyfriends

Hot romcoms that will make you laugh and make you swoon.

Book Boyfriend

Cocky Roommate

Hot Single Dad

## The Always Series

Smoking hot, dirty talking bad boys with some angsty intensity.

Always Have

Always Will

Always Ever After

# ABOUT THE AUTHOR

Claire Kingsley writes smart, sexy romances with sassy heroines, swoony heroes who love their women hard, panty-melting sexytimes, romantic happily ever afters, and all the big feels.

She can't imagine life without coffee, her Kindle, and the sexy heroes who inhabit her imagination. She's living out her own happily ever after in the Pacific Northwest with her husband and three kids.

www.clairekingsleybooks.com

Made in the USA
Middletown, DE
05 December 2021

54366239R00144